Side Show

Book & Lyrics by
Bill Russell

Music by
Henry Krieger

Additional book material by
Bill Condon

D1716065

A SAMUEL FRENCH ACTING EDITION

SAMUEL
FRENCH
FOUNDED 1830

SAMUELFRENCH.COM
SAMUELFRENCH-LONDON.CO.UK

Book & Lyrics Copyright © 1994, 1999, 2016 by Bill Russell
Music Copyright © 1994, 1999, 2016 by Henry Krieger
All Rights Reserved

SIDE SHOW is fully protected under the copyright laws of the United States of America, the British Commonwealth, including Canada, and all other countries of the Copyright Union. All rights, including professional and amateur stage productions, recitation, lecturing, public reading, motion picture, radio broadcasting, television and the rights of translation into foreign languages are strictly reserved.

ISBN 978-0-573-70484-0

www.SamuelFrench.com
www.SamuelFrench-London.co.uk

FOR PRODUCTION ENQUIRIES

UNITED STATES AND CANADA
Info@Samuelfrench.com
1-866-598-8449

UNITED KINGDOM AND EUROPE
Plays@SamuelFrench-London.co.uk
020-7255-4302

Each title is subject to availability from Samuel French, depending upon country of performance. Please be aware that *SIDE SHOW* may not be licensed by Samuel French in your territory. Professional and amateur producers should contact the nearest Samuel French office or licensing partner to verify availability.

CAUTION: Professional and amateur producers are hereby warned that *SIDE SHOW* is subject to a licensing fee. Publication of this play(s) does not imply availability for performance. Both amateurs and professionals considering a production are strongly advised to apply to Samuel French before starting rehearsals, advertising, or booking a theatre. A licensing fee must be paid whether the title(s) is presented for charity or gain and whether or not admission is charged. Professional/Stock licensing fees are quoted upon application to Samuel French.

No one shall make any changes in this title(s) for the purpose of production. No part of this book may be reproduced, stored in a retrieval system, or transmitted in any form, by any means, now known or yet to be invented, including mechanical, electronic, photocopying, recording, videotaping, or otherwise, without the prior written permission of the publisher. No one shall upload this title(s), or part of this title(s), to any social media websites.

For all enquiries regarding motion picture, television, and other media rights, please contact Samuel French.

MUSIC USE NOTE

Licensees are solely responsible for obtaining formal written permission from copyright owners to use copyrighted music in the performance of this play and are strongly cautioned to do so. If no such permission is obtained by the licensee, then the licensee must use only original music that the licensee owns and controls. Licensees are solely responsible and liable for all music clearances and shall indemnify the copyright owners of the play(s) and their licensing agent, Samuel French, against any costs, expenses, losses and liabilities arising from the use of music by licensees. Please contact the appropriate music licensing authority in your territory for the rights to any incidental music.

IMPORTANT BILLING AND CREDIT REQUIREMENTS

If you have obtained performance rights to this title, please refer to your licensing agreement for important billing and credit requirements.

The 2014 Broadway Revival of *SIDE SHOW* was originally directed by Bill Condon and produced by Darren Bagert, Martin Massman, Jayne Baron Sherman, Joan Raffe & Jhett Tolentino, Universal Stage Productions, Joined At the Hip Productions, CJ E&M/Mike Coolik, Shadowcatcher Entertainment, Michael M. Kaiser, Jim Kierstead, Marc David Levine, Catherine & Fred Adler, Bredeweg & Carlberg, Clear Channel Spectacolor, Curtis Forsythe, Gloken, Highbrow & Nahem, Nobile Lehner Shea Productions, Pretty Freaks, Weatherby & Fishman Theatrical, Matthew Masten, and Jujamcyn Theaters, in association with The John F. Kennedy Center for The Performing Arts & La Jolla Playhouse. The cast was as follows

VIOLET HILTON . . . . Erin Davie

DAISY HILTON . . . . Emily Padgett

TERRY CONNOR . . . . Ryan Silverman

BUDDY FOSTER . . . . Matthew Hydzik

JAKE. . . . . David St. Louis

SIR. . . . . Robert Joy

3-LEGGED MAN, SUITOR. . . . . Brandon Bieber

GEEK, DOCTOR . . . . Matthew Patrick Davis

FORTUNE TELLER. . . . . Charity Angél Dawson

VENUS DE MILO. . . . . .Lauren Elder

DOG BOY, HOUDINI, SUITOR . . . . Javier Ignacio

FEMALE COSSACK . . . . .Jordanna James

HALF MAN/HALF WOMAN, DOCTOR. . . . . Kelvin Moon Loh

HUMAN PIN CUSHION, JUDGE, RAY, SUITOR. . . . . Barett Martin

LIZARD MAN, DOCTOR, SIR'S LAWYER,
CAMERAMAN, TOD BROWNING . . . . Don Richard

BEARDED LADY, AUNTIE. . . . . .Blair Ross

TATTOO GIRL . . . . Hannah Shankman

MALE COSSACK . . . . .Josh Walker

ROUSTABOUT, DOCTOR, SUITOR. . . . . .Derek Hanson

ROUSTABOUT, SUITOR. . . . . .Con O'Shea-Creal

SUITOR. . . . . Michaeljon Slinger

ENSEMBLE . . . . Brandon Bieber, Matthew Patrick Davis,
Charity Angél Dawson, Lauren Elder, Derek Hanson,
Javier Ignacio, Jordanna James, Kelvin Moon Loh, Barrett Martin,
Con O'Shea-Creal, Don Richard, Blair Ross, Hannah Shankman, Josh
Walker

The 1997 Broadway Production of *SIDE SHOW* was originally directed and choreographed by Robert Longbottom and produced by Emanuel Azenberg, Joseph Nederlander, Herschel Waxman, Janice McKenna, and Scott Nederlander.

CHARACTERS

VIOLET HILTON

DAISY HILTON

TERRY CONNOR

BUDDY FOSTER

JAKE

SIR

SIR'S LAWYER

3-LEGGED MAN

GEEK

FORTUNE TELLER

VENUS DE MILO

DOG BOY

HOUDINI

FEMALE COSSACK

MALE COSSACK

HALF MAN/HALF WOMAN

HUMAN PIN CUSHION

JUDGE

RAY

LIZARD MAN

CAMERAMAN

TOD BROWNING

BEARDED LADY

AUNTIE

TATTOO GIRL

DOCTORS (4)

SUITORS (6)

ROUSTABOUTS (2)

+ ENSEMBLE

ACT I

Scene 1
Outside/Inside The Tent

[MUSIC NO. 1: "COME LOOK AT THE FREAKS."]

(**TERRY** *is revealed staring at a poster of the movie* "Freaks.")

(*Voices, as if from a distant memory, are heard.*)

ALL.

COME LOOK AT THE FREAKS
THE PYGMIES AND GEEKS
COME EXAMINE THESE ABERRATIONS
THEIR MALFORMATIONS
GROTESQUE PHYSIQUES
ONLY PENNIES FOR PEEKS
COME LOOK AT THE FREAKS

MEN.

COME LOOK AT THE FREAKS	**WOMEN.**
THEY'LL HAUNT YOU FOR WEEKS	AH... AH... COME...

COME EXPLORE WHY THEY
    FASCINATE YOU
EXASPERATE YOU
AND FLUSH YOUR CHEEKS

WOMEN.

COME HEAR HOW LOVE SPEAKS.

ALL.

COME LOOK AT THE FREAKS!

(The poster flies out and **TERRY** *exits as* **SIR** *enters.)*

SIR.

LADIES AND GENTLEMEN
STEP RIGHT UP
RIGHT THIS WAY.
THERE IS NO WAIT
WE DON'T WASTE YOUR TIME
SO LITTLE TO PAY
JUST ONE THIN DIME
GAINS YOU ADMISSION
TO MY ODDITORIUM

NEVER HAVE YOU SEEN
A COMP'RABLE EMPORIUM
OF WONDERS UNDER ONE TENT
YOUR DIME COULD NOT BE BETTER SPENT

*(***ATTRACTIONS*** are revealed as* **SIR** *describes them.)*

COME, SEE A CURIOUS GAL,
THE BEARDED LADY
SEE A MAN WITH AN EXTRA APPENDAGE
INSTEAD OF TWO LEGS, THERE'S THREE
COME SEE OUR TATTOOED GIRL
SHE'S A WALKING MARQUEE

COME SEE OUR ELEGANT GEEK
REFINED BUT DEADLY.
CHICKEN NECKS DELIGHT HIS INCISORS
THEIR HEADS DECORATE THE MUD
HIS FAV'RITE COCKTAIL DRINK?
IT'S WARM CHICKEN BLOOD!

FROM THE BARREN DESERT
OF THE HEATHEN CAMEL TRADE
THE LIZARD MAN OF KHARTOUM
AN ENCOUNTER WITH HIM WILL MEAN CERTAIN DOOM
AND FROM THE FAR EAST

SEE THIS INTRIGUING SPECIMEN
IS IT WOMAN? IS IT MAN?
I GUESS YOU'LL BE SATISFIED EITHER WAY
WITH HALF AND HALF FROM SAIPAN!

COME HAVE YOUR FORTUNE FORETOLD!

>   (**FORTUNE TELLER** *dances.*)

THEN SEE A BOY WHO'S A DOG

>   (**DOG BOY** *howls.*)

THE LIVING VENUS DE MILO, LACKING BOTH ARMS

>   (**LIVING VENUS** *smokes a cigarette with her toes.*)

And from the Siberian tundra – the world's tiniest
Cossacks!

>   (**MALE & FEMALE COSSACKS** *dance.*)

He's punctured! He's pierced! He's the human pin
cushion!

>   (**HUMAN PIN CUSHION** *sticks a long needle
>   through his arm.*)

ALL.
COME SEE GOD'S MISTAKES!
THE FREAKS GOD FORSAKES
TAKE A LOOK AT EXOTIC CREATURES
THEIR MANGLED FEATURES
THE MESS GOD MAKES

SIR.
AND WE DON'T HARBOR FAKES!

ALL.
COME SEE GOD'S MISTAKES

>   (**JAKE**, *an African-American man, enters in
>   shackles, held on either side by* **ROUSTABOUTS**.)

SIR.
FROM THE INKY JUNGLES
OF THE DARKEST CONTINENT
TIME TO WITNESS FIRST HAND
THE FEROCITY OF THE CANNIBAL KING
WE KEEP HIM CHAINED UP

SIR. *(Cont.)*
> BECAUSE WE KNOW HE'S HANKERING
> FOR A TASTE OF ONE OF YOU
> AND YOU ARE HERE FOR ENLIGHTENMENT
> NOT FOR STOCK IN CANNIBAL STEW

>> **(CANNIBAL** *breaks free. He is "captured" by* **ROUSTABOUTS.***)*

> Please remain calm – no cause for alarm – the Cannibal King has been subdued and is under our control. There is nothing to fear. And now for our premiere attraction.

>> *(***DAISY** *and* **VIOLET** *are revealed in silhouette.)*

> LADIES AND GENTLEMEN
> WITH GREAT PRIDE,
> MISTY-EYED,
> I NOW PRESENT
> THE STARS OF OUR SHOW
> NO DUO IS MORE SIMPATICO
> THOUGH THEIR CONDITION
> IS CALLED "ABNORMALITY"
> THEY'VE DEVELOPED CHARM
> AND GIFTS OF MUSICALITY
> THEIR BOND IMMUTABLY STRONG
> JUST LISTEN TO THEIR HAUNTING SONG

DAISY & VIOLET.
> AH…
> AH…
> AH…

>> *(The* **ATTRACTIONS** *underscore with "AHH" throughout* **SIR***'s dialogue.)*

SIR. Scientists believe that Siamese twins come from the same life germ and that their complete separation was retarded in some way – perhaps, while pregnant, their mother witnessed dogs stuck together copulating. They are called "Siamese" after Chang and Eng, the first widely known specimens.

SIR. Siamese twins share everything – yet remain completely separate in their minds, bodily functions and, presumably, their souls. But enough about science. Sing, girls, sing!

DAISY & VIOLET. *(Now in full view.)*
>AH AH AH
>AH AH AH AH
>AH

SIR. Come look at the freaks!

ALL.
>SPREAD THE WORD!

SIR. The pygmies and geeks!

ALL.
>TELL THE WORLD
>WHAT YOU'VE SEEN AND
>HEARD

SIR & ALL.
>COME EXAMINE THESE ABERRATIONS
>THEIR MALFORMATIONS
>GROTESQUE PHYSIQUES

SIR.
>ONLY PENNIES FOR PEEKS!

SIR & ALL.
>COME LOOK AT THE FREAKS!

>*(Scene change.)*

Scene 2
On The Midway

[MUSIC NO. 1A: "FREAKS PLAYOFF."]

*(***TERRY*** *enters. The* **TATTOO GIRL** *emerges from the shadows passing him suggestively – a distraction while the* **HUMAN PIN CUSHION** *lifts his wallet.* **BUDDY** *enters and* **TATTOO GIRL** *and* **PIN CUSHION** *recede back into the shadows.)*

BUDDY. I took two trains, a bus and a streetcar to see a freak show? What's next, Terry, strippers and cock fights?

TERRY. Nothing's next. This is it.

BUDDY. I thought the whole point of meeting you in Texas was to scout some new acts.

TERRY. Those girls, Buddy – the twins. You didn't find them intriguing? Exciting?

BUDDY. Unnerving is more like it. I had the weirdest feeling when I was watching them. It was like they were the ones watching me.

TERRY. Exactly. That connection they make to an audience – it's incredible…as rare as snow on the Alamo.

BUDDY. No, I'm not hearing this.

TERRY. Buddy, they've got potential. You could teach them to really sing. Show them some steps.

BUDDY. Terry, you need to get back to New York and real entertainers.

TERRY. You know I can't do that.

BUDDY. Look, I've been talking to the boys down at the Orpheum home office…

TERRY. Screw the Orpheum!

*(***SIR*** *enters.)*

SIR. That was our last show today. Unless…would you gentlemen like to see more?

TERRY. More?

SIR. Of the Siamese twins, for example. Sometimes I'm able to convince them to reveal their connection for those with a scientific interest in their condition. Of course, a small consideration would be helpful. Two bucks allows total exposure of the fleshy link. And don't get any ideas. These girls are my daughters – so, look all you want, but no touching!

[MUSIC NO. 1B: "BEHIND THE TENT."]

(**TERRY** *goes for his wallet only to discover it missing.* **BUDDY** *hands over the two bucks.* **SIR** *indicates for them to follow him.*)

(*Scene change.*)

Scene 3
Behind The Tent

*(DAISY and VIOLET are folding laundry. A fight
erupts over a card game. The MALE COSSACK
runs from the fight and knocks over the laundry
basket, spilling the contents on the ground.)*

JAKE. Daisy! Violet!

*(DAISY and VIOLET turn from picking up the
laundry as the GEEK and others present a surprise
birthday cake to them.)*

ALL. *(Ad lib.)* Happy Birthday! To you and to you! Many
happy returns!

(SIR enters followed by TERRY & BUDDY.)

SIR. Okay. Good news. The Twins have a private
appointment.

GEEK. But it's their birthday.

SIR. Looks like they have to wash that laundry again. So,
after you're examined by these gentlemen, you'll finish
your chores –

(To GEEK.)

And then we can all have some of your delicious cake.

*(The ATTRACTIONS back into the shadows but
keep watching. BUDDY also keeps his distance.)*

JAKE. Boss, the day's receipts are in the tin and there's a
new bottle in the larder.

SIR. Good. You stay here, Jake. Mister, you got ten minutes.

(Exits.)

DAISY. *(To VIOLET, starting to unbutton her dress.)* Happy
birthday.

VIOLET. *(To DAISY, also unbuttoning.)* Happy birthday.

TERRY. Wait. You don't have to show me anything. I just
want to talk.

JAKE. You made a deal to look, not talk.

TERRY. I only want a couple minutes of private conversation.

VIOLET. He seems okay, Jake.

JAKE. *(Relenting, to* **TERRY**.*)* I'm keeping an eye on you.

> *(He moves away but remains visible.)*

TERRY. *(To the twins.)* Name's Terry Connor. What are yours?

[MUSIC NO. 1C: "I'M DAISY. I'M VIOLET."]

DAISY.

> I'M DAISY

VIOLET.

> I'M VIOLET

DAISY & VIOLET.

> WE'RE SIAMESE TWINS

TERRY. So I noticed. What's that like?

VIOLET. Oh, it's a real picnic.

DAISY. What's it like being handsome?

VIOLET. You're being rude.

DAISY. Am not.

TERRY. I was rude to ask.

VIOLET. Everyone does.

TERRY. They're just fascinated. You're exactly alike. I'm sorry, which one is…?

DAISY.

> I'M DAISY

VIOLET.

> I'M VIOLET

DAISY & VIOLET.

> WE'RE NOTHING ALIKE

VIOLET.

> I'M TO YOUR RIGHT
> AS YOU WATCH OUR SHOW

DAISY.

> SHE THINKS SHE'S ALWAYS RIGHT

DAISY & VIOLET.

> NOT SO

DAISY.

> I'M DAISY

VIOLET.

> I'M VIOLET

DAISY & VIOLET.

> WHAT ELSE WOULD YOU LIKE TO KNOW?

TERRY. I'm intrigued by your singing. You're not without talent. And potential.

DAISY. But we're freaks.

TERRY. Not the word I'd use. You're exotic! Special and rare! I want to know everything about you. Where did you come from? How do you manage? What do you want for your birthday?

> (**VIOLET** *looks to* **DAISY**, *who nods.* **VIOLET** *takes a deep breath.*)

> ### *[MUSIC NO. 2: "LIKE EVERYONE ELSE."]*

VIOLET.

> I WANT TO BE LIKE EV'RYONE ELSE
> SO NO ONE WILL POINT AND STARE
> TO WALK DOWN THE STREET
> NOT ATTRACTING ATTENTION
> NO NOTICE, NO MENTION
> NO HINT OF DESPAIR
> A NORMAL REACTION
> A STANDARD RESPONSE
> THE SAME AS EVERYONE WANTS

DAISY.

> I WANT TO BE LIKE EV'RYONE ELSE
> BUT RICHER AND MORE ACCLAIMED
> WORSHIPPED AND CELEBRATED
> PAMPERED AND LOVED
> TO SEE THOSE WHO'VE LAUGHED
> FEELING ASHAMED
> A GLORIOUS, FRANTIC
> ADORING RESPONSE
> THE SAME AS EVERYONE WANTS

    I'D GO ABROAD
    SEE ALL THE SIGHTS
    HEAR FOLKS APPLAUD
    BOW TO THE LIGHTS

VIOLET.
    I'D SETTLE DOWN
    NEVER TO ROAM
    FIND A NICE HUSBAND AND HOME
    I WANT TO BE

DAISY.
    I WANT TO BE

DAISY & VIOLET.
    LIKE EVERYONE ELSE
    BUT NOT LIKE MY SISTER SAYS

DAISY.
    SHE WANTS STABILITY

VIOLET.
    SHE WOULD LIKE FAME
    I'D LIKE SERENITY

DAISY.
    FRENZIED ACCLAIM

DAISY & VIOLET.
    THOUGH WE CAN'T AGREE
    ON A SINGLE RESPONSE
    WE WANT WHAT EV'RYONE WANTS
    ONLY WHAT EV'RYONE WANTS
    THE SAME AS EV'RYONE WANTS

DAISY. This is fun. Our turn.

TERRY. For what?

VIOLET. To ask questions.

DAISY & VIOLET. Why are you here?

TERRY. I'm a talent scout and press agent for the Orpheum circuit.

        (**BUDDY** *gives him a look, knowing* **TERRY** *is lying.*)

I think you girls could play vaudeville.

DAISY. Vaudeville!

VIOLET. We're side show exhibits. People like us don't perform in places like that.

TERRY. Are you kidding? Every vaudeville star is…unusual in some way.

VIOLET. You mean a freak?

TERRY. Again, that's your term, not mine – but people don't pay to see the ordinary. Sophie Tucker,

[MUSIC NO. 3: "VERY WELL-CONNECTED."]

Fanny Brice, W.C. Fields – they're all…unique.

DAISY. *(To* **VIOLET**.*)* I guess now we're…

DAISY & VIOLET. "Unique."

TERRY. And I know how to sell that!

    I'M THE GUY
    WHO BOOKS THE STARS
    TO PLAY THE SHOWS
    THAT GARNER THE BRAVISSIMOS
    AND FILL THE ROWS
    OF THEATERS
    IN LEXINGTONS AND BUFFALOS
    WITH ACTS I'VE PRE-SELECTED
    I'M VERY WELL-CONNECTED

DAISY. So are we.

TERRY. I love that you can laugh at your situation – no self-pity. Buddy, come here. This is Buddy Foster – vocal coach, dance master, miracle worker.

BUDDY. I'm a performer too.

TERRY.

    I CAN SEE YOU ON A STAGE
    FOOT-LIGHTS AGLOW
    ATOP A VAUDEVILLE OLIO
    YOU'D LEAD THE BILL AS CRITICS CROW
    THANKS TO YOUR IMPRESARIO
    WHO HAS HIS GAME PERFECTED
    I'M VERY WELL-CONNECTED

> I KNOW THE BIG PRODUCERS
> AND ALL THE V.I.P.'S

DAISY & VIOLET. Like who?

TERRY.

> ANYONE WHO'S ANYONE
> ARE FRIENDS OR ENEMIES
> I'M ON A FIRST-NAME BASIS
> WITH THE LAUDED AND RESPECTED
> THE SELF-MADE KINGS
> WHO PULL THE STRINGS
> I'M VERY WELL-CONNECTED

BUDDY. Terry, could I speak to you a minute?

TERRY. Now?

BUDDY. Yes.

TERRY. *(To* **DAISY & VIOLET.***)* Excuse me, ladies.

> *(Crossing reluctantly to* **BUDDY***.)*

What the hell? You're messing up my rhythm.

BUDDY. I'm a song and dance man – not a magician.

TERRY. You worked magic for me with the Johnson Brothers.

BUDDY. They weren't joined at the hip!

TERRY. They weren't brothers either! You're always begging me for a chance to perform. Help me turn those girls into stars and I'll make that happen for you. I promise this time.

> *(As he crosses back to the twins.)*

> IT'S MY DREAM
> TO MAKE YOUR DREAM REALITY
> NOW WILL YOU COME ALONG WITH ME?
> I'D LIKE TO SEE YOU ALL SUCCEED
> AND END UP WHERE YOU LONG TO BE
> WITH MORE THAN YOU EXPECTED
> I'M VERY WELL-CONNECTED

BUDDY.

    SEE A MASTER PLY HIS TRADE

    WHAT A POWER TO PERSUADE

    WE ALL MIGHT HAVE IT MADE

    BY MAKING THIS CONNECTION

    HE'S OUR TICKET TO THE TOP

    OUR PIECE OF CAKE, OUR LOLLIPOP

    LET'S TAKE THIS RIDE AND NEVER STOP

    WHAT A POWERFUL CONNECTION

TERRY.

    I HOPE THAT I'LL BE WORKING

    WITH YOU AND YOU AND YOU

TERRY & BUDDY.

    WE'RE A TEAM WHO'S GOT A DREAM

BUDDY.

    WHO KNOWS WHAT WE CAN DO?

TERRY & BUDDY.

    WE'LL MAKE OUR WAY TOGETHER

    WITH PARTNERS WE'VE COLLECTED

BUDDY.

    WE'RE VERY WELL

TERRY.

    EXTREMELY WELL

TERRY.	**BUDDY.**
VERY	
WELL	VERY
WELL	WELL

TERRY & BUDDY.

    CONNECTED

JAKE. Okay, time's up. Mister, you'd better get out of here.

DAISY. No, Jake! Let him stay.

       *(***DAISY*** nudges* **VIOLET***.)*

VIOLET. For me, Jake?

JAKE. Violet, that's not fair.

DAISY. *(To* **TERRY***.)* He can't say no to her.

TERRY. Good man. So here's my plan. Buddy will teach you a song. Some sweet little ditty…like…like – hey, Buddy, what about that number your Darling Damsels do? "Normal Girls…"

BUDDY. "Typical Girls Next Door"?

TERRY. That's it!

VIOLET. "Typical Girls"? Us? But Sir will never allow it.

DAISY. We can work late at night after he passes out.

BUDDY. It'll be fun to teach you a number.

DAISY. I'm a quick learner.

TERRY. Great! My kind of girl.

VIOLET. You'd have your work cut out with me.

BUDDY. You've got more charm just standing still than a lot of the people I've taught to dance.

TERRY. No pressure. You'll sing a song for us and maybe some of your friends.

BUDDY. Nothing to worry about.

TERRY. Will you girls do as we tell you and work very hard?

VIOLET. I'll try.

DAISY. Anything you say.

> *[MUSIC NO. 3A: "BEFORE DEVIL YOU KNOW."]*

TERRY.
> SAY GOOD-BYE TO THE SIDE SHOW
> LET ME SHOW YOU A PLACE I KNOW

BUDDY.
> WHERE ONLY DAISIES AND VI'LETS GROW

JAKE. Oh my God…

TERRY & BUDDY.
> SAY GOOD-BYE TO THE SIDE SHOW

JAKE.
> GOOD-BYE

> *(**TERRY**, **BUDDY** and **JAKE** exit.)*

DAISY.

> WHAT BROUGHT HIM HERE
> THAT HANDSOME GUY?

VIOLET.

> I GUESS HIS SCHEME
> IS WORTH A TRY

DAISY.

> DO YOU THINK HE COULD MAKE
> OUR DREAMS COME TRUE?

VIOLET.

> HE SURE WOULD HAVE A LOT OF WORK TO DO
>
> *(The* **ATTRACTIONS** *start emerging.)*

FORTUNE TELLER.

> HE'S THE ONE TO DO IT
> I CAN SEE IT ALL.
> SEE IT IN MY CRYSTAL BALL.

DAISY. You heard what he said?

FEMALE COSSACK. Every word.

THREE LEGGED MAN. We all did.

BEARDED LADY.

> DAISY AND VI'LET
> PLEASE DON'T GO WITH THEM

TATTOO GIRL.

> NO! GIVE THEM A TRY

DAISY.

> WE'VE ALREADY AGREED TO

VIOLET.

> AGREED TO LEARN A SONG
> NOT TO LEAVE YOU

LIZARD MAN.

> NOT YET

HALF MAN/HALF WOMAN.

> IT'S CLEAR WHAT HE SAID
> "SAY GOOD-BYE TO THE SIDE SHOW"

VIOLET.

> I WOULD NEVER DO THAT

DAISY.

    I WOULD

    NOT BECAUSE I WANT TO LEAVE YOU

    BUT TO PLAY VAUDEVILLE

    TO MAKE SOMETHING OF OUR LIVES

LITTLE WOMAN.

    THIS LIFE ISN'T GOOD ENOUGH FOR YOU?

TATTOO GIRL.

    YOU CALL THIS A LIFE?

GEEK.

    I CALL THIS THE ONLY HOME

    THE GIRLS HAVE EVER KNOWN

THREE LEGGED MAN.

    PREDATORS WILL TARGET THEM

    OUT THERE ON THEIR OWN

HALF MAN/HALF WOMAN.

    WELL, I THINK THEY SHOULD GO

JAKE. *(enters)*

    THAT'S ENOUGH!

    THIS IS NOT ABOUT ANY OF US

    THIS IS THEIR DECISION

[MUSIC NO. 4: "THE DEVIL YOU KNOW."]

    I'M NOT GONNA TELL YOU

    YOU'RE MAKING A MISTAKE

    TELL YOU NOT TO GO

    NO, I WON'T

    I'LL ONLY SAY

    WHAT I'VE LEARNED ALONG MY WAY

    THE DEVIL YOU KNOW

    BEATS THE DEVIL YOU DON'T

    WE DON'T WORK

    IN THE BEST OF SITUATIONS

    WE DON'T LIVE VERY WELL

    DON'T RESIDE

    IN THE NEIGHBORHOOD OF HEAVEN

    WE LIVE SOMEWHERE CLOSER TO HELL

JAKE. *(Cont.)*
>
> WE HAVE LEARNED
> TO WORK AROUND THIS SITUATION
> LEARNED TO HIDE
> TILL THE HEAT HAS PASSED
> YOU WILL LEARN
> A PROMISE OF SALVATION
> CAN MASK ANOTHER INFERNO'S BLAST
>
> THE DEVIL YOU KNOW
> BEATS THE DEVIL YOU DON'T
> THAT PROMISED LAND
> COULD TURN OUT TO BE DRY
> ONCE YOU'RE GONE
> YOU MIGHT ASK YOURSELVES WHY
> MAYBE YOU WILL
> OR MAYBE YOU WON'T
> BUT THE DEVIL YOU KNOW
> BEATS THE DEVIL YOU DON'T

LIZARD MAN.
>
> NO YOU DON'T KNOW
> THE WORLD BEYOND THE SIDE SHOW

HUMAN PIN CUSHION.
>
> YOU DON'T KNOW
> WHAT SATAN CAN PLAN

BEARDED LADY.
>
> YOU DON'T KNOW
> THE SAFETY YOU'D BE LEAVING

DOG BOY.
>
> WE'RE YOUR FAM'LY
> WE'RE YOUR CLAN

VENUS DE MILO.
>
> HERE WE'VE GOT
> EACH OTHER TO DEPEND ON

LITTLE MALE.
>
> HERE YOU'VE GOT
> THE BEST HOME YOU'LL EVER FIND

BEARDED LADY.
>   OTHER FOLK
>   DON'T KNOW HOW TO TAKE US

JAKE.
>   THE WORLD OUT THERE
>   CAN BE SO UNKIND

JAKE.
>   THE DEVIL YOU KNOW

LIZARD MAN. *(Overlapping.)*
>   DEVIL YOU KNOW

PIN CUSHION. *(Overlapping.)*
>   DEVIL YOU KNOW

JAKE. *(Overlapping.)*
>   BEATS THE DEVIL YOU DON'T

VENUS DE MILO, BEARDED LADY, MALE COSSACK, PIN CUSHION & LIZARD MAN.
>   BEATS THE DEVIL
>   THE DEVIL YOU DON'T

JAKE.
>   HIS GAME OF CHANCE

DOG BOY.
>   DON'T TAKE THAT CHANCE

JAKE.
>   JUST MIGHT BE A SCAM

DOG BOY, VENUS, BEARDED LADY.
>   IT'S JUST A SCAM

JAKE, PIN CUSHION.
>   YOU CAN'T PLAY
>   THEN DECIDE YOU SHOULD SCRAM

JAKE, PIN CUSHION, LIZARD MAN & FEMALE COSSACK.
>   MAYBE YOU'LL WIN
>   OR MAYBE YOU WON'T

JAKE, DOG BOY & BEARDED LADY.
>   BUT THE DEVIL YOU KNOW

PIN CUSHION, LIZARD MAN.
>   DEVIL YOU KNOW

JAKE, MALE & FEMALE COSSACKS, VENUS DE MILO,
PIN-CUSHION MAN, BEARDED LADY, LIZARD MAN & DOG BOY.
>   BEATS THE DEVIL YOU DON'T

TATTOO GIRL.
>   HOW CAN YOU
>   SAY THAT MAN'S A DEVIL?

HALF MAN/HALF WOMAN.
>   HOW CAN YOU
>   SAY HE'S WICKED AND BAD?

GEEK.
>   HOW CAN YOU
>   CRITICIZE AN ANGEL?

ALL THREE.
>   PROMISING MORE HEAVEN
>   THAN THEY'VE EVER HAD

FORTUNE TELLER.
>   I'M A FORTUNE TELLER
>   I CAN SEE THE FUTURE
>   I CAN LOOK AT PEOPLE
>   SEE WHAT'S LYING AHEAD
>
>   VIOLET AND DAISY
>   I SEE YOU'RE BOUND FOR GLORY
>   THE MAN THAT WAS HERE
>   WILL DO ALL THAT HE SAID
>
>   THAT MAN'S NOT A DEVIL
>   NO! I KNOW THAT HE'S NOT
>   I'VE SEEN THE DEVIL, WHOA…
>   YOU GIRLS CAN GET
>   MUCH MORE THAN YOU'VE GOT
>   MUCH MORE, MUCH MORE THAN YOU'VE GOT!

JAKE, PIN-CUSHION MAN, VENUS, BEARDED LADY, LIZARD
MAN, DOG BOY & MALE & FEMALE COSSACKS.
>   WHAT IF HE'S A DEVIL?

FORTUNE TELLER. *(Overlapping with above.)*
>   GO!

TATTOO GIRL, ROUSTABOUT #1 & #2, THREE LEGGED MAN & HALF/HALF WOMAN.

WHAT IF HE'S NOT?

HE COULD BE AN ANGEL

JAKE, PIN-CUSHION MAN, VENUS, BEARDED LADY, LIZARD MAN, DOG BOY & MALE & FEMALE COSSACKS.

THAT HEAVEN FORGOT!

FORTUNE TELLER.

I THINK YOU MAY BE JEALOUS

JAKE.

JEALOUS OF WHAT?

TATTOO GIRL, FORTUNE TELLER, ROUSTABOUT #1 & #2, THREE LEGGED MAN & HALF/HALF WOMAN.

THAT VIOLET AND DAISY

MIGHT GIVE HIM A SHOT!

JAKE, PIN-CUSHION MAN, VENUS, BEARDED LADY, LIZARD MAN, DOG BOY & MALE & FEMALE COSSACKS.

THE DEVIL YOU KNOW

TATTOO GIRL, FORTUNE TELLER, ROUSTABOUT #1 & #2, THREE LEGGED MAN & HALF/HALF WOMAN.

HE'S NOT A DEVIL

JAKE, PIN-CUSHION MAN, VENUS, BEARDED LADY, LIZARD MAN, DOG BOY & MALE & FEMALE COSSACK.

BEATS THE DEVIL YOU DON'T

TATTOO GIRL, FORTUNE TELLER, ROUSTABOUT #1 & #2, THREE LEGGED MAN & HALF/HALF WOMAN.

I WON'T BELEIVE IT

BELIEVE IT I WON'T

JAKE, PIN-CUSHION MAN, VENUS, BEARDED LADY, LIZARD MAN, DOG BOY & MALE & FEMALE COSSACKS.

THAT PROMISED LAND

TATTOO GIRL, FORTUNE TELLER, ROUSTABOUT #1 & #2, THREE LEGGED MAN & HALF/HALF WOMAN.

IS AT HAND

JAKE, PIN-CUSHION MAN, VENUS, BEARDED LADY, LIZARD MAN, DOG BOY & MALE & FEMALE COSSACKS.

COULD TURN OUT TO BE DRY

TATTOO GIRL, FORTUNE TELLER, ROUSTABOUT #1 & #2, THREE LEGGED MAN & HALF/HALF WOMAN.

YOU SHOULD GIVE IT A TRY

JAKE, PIN-CUSHION MAN, VENUS, BEARDED LADY, LIZARD MAN, DOG BOY & MALE & FEMALE COSSACKS.

SO DRY—

ONCE YOU'RE GONE YOU MIGHT

ASK YOURSELVES WHY

TATTOO GIRL, FORTUNE TELLER, ROUSTABOUT #1 & #2, THREE LEGGED MAN & HALF/HALF WOMAN.

WHY?

ALL.

MAYBE YOU WILL

OR MAYBE YOU WON'T

JAKE, PIN-CUSHION MAN, VENUS, BEARDED LADY, LIZARD MAN, DOG BOY & MALE & FEMALE COSSACKS.

BUT THE DEVIL YOU KNOW

TATTOO GIRL, FORTUNE TELLER, ROUSTABOUT #1 & #2, THREE LEGGED MAN & HALF/HALF WOMAN.

NO! NO! HE'S NOT A DEVIL!

JAKE, PIN-CUSHION MAN, VENUS, BEARDED LADY, LIZARD MAN, DOG BOY & MALE & FEMALE COSSACKS.

BUT THE DEVIL YOU KNOW

TATTOO GIRL, FORTUNE TELLER, ROUSTABOUT #1 & #2, THREE LEGGED MAN & HALF/HALF WOMAN.

NO! NO! HE'S NOT A DEVIL!

JAKE, PIN-CUSHION MAN, VENUS, BEARDED LADY, LIZARD MAN, DOG BOY & MALE & FEMALE COSSACKS.

BUT THE DEVIL YOU KNOW

TATTOO GIRL, FORTUNE TELLER, ROUSTABOUT #1 & #2, THREE LEGGED MAN & HALF/HALF WOMAN.

NO! NO! HE'S NOT A DEVIL!

JAKE.

ALRIGHT

NOW WE COULD ARGUE ALL NIGHT

BECAUSE WE CARE ABOUT YOU TWO

MAYBE YOU WILL GO

OR MAYBE YOU WON'T
BUT I HOPE YOU WILL REMEMBER
THAT THAT MEAN OLD
MONEY-GRUBBIN'
GIN-GUZZLIN'
NAME-CALLIN'
DEVIL YOU KNOW
MIGHT BE BETTER THAN
A SMOOTH-TALKIN'
FINE-LOOKIN'
DREAM-SPINNIN'
PROMISE MAKIN' DEVIL
YOU DON'T!

TATTOO GIRL, FORTUNE TELLER, ROUSTABOUT #1 & #2, THREE LEGGED MAN & HALF/HALF WOMAN.

NO, NO, NO,

TATTOO GIRL, FORTUNE TELLER, ROUSTABOUT #1 & #2, THREE LEGGED MAN & HALF/HALF WOMAN.	**JAKE, PIN-CUSHION MAN, VENUS, BEARDED LADY, LIZARD MAN, DOG BOY & MALE & FEMALE COSSACKS.**
DON'T CALL HIM A DEVIL!	BEATS THE DEVIL YOU DON'T
NO, NO, NO,	
DON'T CALL HIM A DEVIL!	BEATS THE DEVIL YOU DON'T
NO, NO, NO,	
DON'T CALL HIM A DEVIL!	BEATS THE DEVIL YOU

ALL.

DON'T!

(On applause, the **ATTRACTIONS** *exit upstage as the set changes to the inside of the tent.)*

Scene 4
Inside The Tent

[MUSIC NO. 4A: "LADIES AND GENTLE-MAN..."]

(**BUDDY** *imitates Sir as the* **ATTRACTIONS** *gather.*)

BUDDY.

LADIES AND GENTLEMEN
STEP RIGHT UP
THOUGH IT'S LATE
YOU WON'T REGRET
THE EFFORT YOU MADE
WE'VE BEEN REHEARSING
SECRETLY MEETING HERE
AND TONIGHT'S THE NIGHT
WE OFFER THE TWINS' PREMIERE
A PRIVATE, EXCLUSIVE SHOW
IN A TENT IN SAN ANTONIO

I'll admit I was uncomfortable when Terry first brought me here, but over the past few weeks you've made me feel right at home.

FEMALE COSSACK. You're just as weird as the rest of us.

BUDDY. Maybe even weirder. It's been a real pleasure working with these lovely girls. And we're thrilled to share what they've achieved. Ladies and Gentlemen, and you who are both, I give you – Daisy and Violet Hilton!

(**DAISY** *and* **VIOLET** *enter and perform.*)

[MUSIC NO. 5: "TYPICAL GIRLS NEXT DOOR."]

DAISY.

AT FIRST GLANCE
YOU MAY THINK WE'RE ABNORMAL

WE MAKE STRIKE YOU
AS DIFF'RENT OR STRANGE

VIOLET.
BUT OUR MOODS
WHETHER RELAXED
OR FORMAL

DAISY & VIOLET.
ARE WELL WITHIN EV'RYDAY RANGE

WE EAT WITH A FORK
WE SLEEP IN A BED
WE WALK WITH OUR FEET ON THE FLOOR
WE SIT IN A CHAIR
WE EVEN BAKE BREAD
LIKE YOUR TYPICAL GIRLS NEXT DOOR

WE STROLL IN THE PARK
WE WADE IN THE LAKE
WE LOVE TO GO OUT AND EXPLORE
WE ASK DEAR OLD DAD
FOR ALL WE CAN TAKE
LIKE YOUR TYPICAL GIRLS NEXT DOOR

WE SWIM
WE PLAY GOLF!
WE COOK
WE SEW!
AND WE PLAY A MEAN GAME OF TENNIS
A SKILL WE ARE HAPPY TO SHOW

> *(Dance break as they demonstrate their skills at the above.)*

LIKE YOUR TYPICAL GIRLS NEXT DOOR

WE STUDY AT SCHOOL
WE GET PASSING GRADES

VIOLET.
BUT HOMEWORK IS   **DAISY.**
  ALWAYS A BORE   SUCH A BORE

DAISY & VIOLET.
>WE'D RATHER PLAY HEARTS
>OLD MAID OR CHARADES
>SING POPULAR AIRS
>OR SOFT SERENADES
>OR EVEN INDULGE
>IN SWEET ESCAPADES
>LIKE YOUR TYPICAL GIRLS
>TYPICAL GIRLS
>NEXT DOOR!

>>*(At the end of the number the* **ATTRACTIONS** *applaud and cheer.* **TERRY** *and* **BUDDY** *rush to congratulate the twins. Then, without warning,* **SIR** *enters, causing a sudden silence.)*

SIR. What the hell is all this bloody racket?

>*(Seeing* **TERRY.***)*

You. I might have known.

>*(Looking around at* **ATTRACTIONS.***)*

What are you all doing here?

DAISY. They came to see us sing and dance.

VIOLET. Buddy taught us.

SIR. Buddy? Well if Buddy taught you. Hello? You girls get back to your trailer.

DAISY. Don't tell us what to do!

SIR. You are my daughters and you will obey me.

DAISY. You're not our father.

SIR. You, Miss Daisy, are really asking for it.

VIOLET. We're not trying to make trouble.

DAISY. We're leaving the side show.

SIR. Leaving the side show? That's a good one! Giving up your jobs in the middle of a depression.

TERRY. I can get them booked on the Orpheum Circuit.

SIR. Oh, think so? And do you also think you're the first slicked-up con-man to try to steal my premier attraction?

TERRY. I'm not trying to steal anything. You'll get your fair share of whatever they earn.

SIR. How generous. Especially since my "fair share" is one hundred percent. You see, I own these girls.

TERRY. Own them? Hasn't anyone told him this is America?

SIR. I don't need to explain anything to you. The twins are fully aware of their situation. Aren't you, girls?

(Pause. Then **DAISY** *and* **VIOLET** *nod together.)*

Now, I think you owe these…gentlemen an apology for wasting their time. Trying to teach you how to…dance. Violet?

VIOLET. I'm sorry.

SIR. That's my good girl. Daisy?

(Pause. **DAISY** *doesn't respond.* **SIR** *erupts.)*

Daisy!

DAISY. I'm sorry.

SIR. Good. We'd hate for our visitors to think I haven't taught you proper manners.

(To **ATTRACTIONS**.*)*

Now, all of you go to bed. It's nearly time for morning chores.

[MUSIC NO. 5A: "TRANSITION TO FLASHBACK."]

(Slowly, the **ATTRACTIONS** *begin to leave.)*

Jake, lock it down.

(To **TERRY & BUDDY**.*)*

Gentlemen, I'm sure you have more important places to be – even at this late hour.

(Exits.)

TERRY. Ladies.

(Starts to exit with **BUDDY***, then making sure* **SIR** *is gone, he turns back and crosses to* **DAISY & VIOLET**.*)*

TERRY. *(Cont.)* Just tell me one thing.

VIOLET. Haven't you caused enough trouble?

TERRY. Daisy, you said he isn't your father.

DAISY. He's not.

TERRY. But he owns you –?

DAISY. Sir is our legal guardian. We never knew our father.

BUDDY. So Sir married your mother?

DAISY. No one married our mother.

VIOLET. Daisy, that's enough!

DAISY. But maybe they can help us.

VIOLET. No one can help us.

DAISY. How do we know?

VIOLET. This is private.

DAISY. Violet, people have been staring at us from the moment we were born. From the beginning our whole life has been a show.

[MUSIC NO. 6: "FLASHBACK (PART 1)."]

*(A music hall theme is heard in the distance. **DAISY** looks to **VIOLET** and starts. **VIOLET** is tentative at first, then both gain momentum as they relate their story, their thoughts and statements overlapping.)*

We were born in England, and our mother started screaming when she saw us two babies together. She couldn't bear to touch us!

VIOLET. She considered us punishment for her sin of being pregnant and unwed!

DAISY. We were even told she prayed for us to die.

VIOLET. But the mid-wife who delivered us…

DAISY. …She also performed abortions…

VIOLET. We always called her "Auntie."

DAISY. …Legally adopted us and…

DAISY & VIOLET. …took us in.

(**AUNTIE** *appears.* **DAISY** *and* **VIOLET** *become their younger selves.*)

AUNTIE.

WHY DON'T YOU GIRLS
DO AS I SAY?
YOU TAKE A LOT OF WORK
AND I GET NO PAY
BUT YOU EARN A LITTLE KEEP
WHEN I PUT YOU ON DISPLAY
YOU SHOULD THANK ME EVERY DAY

DAISY.

AUNTIE, WE ARE SO HUNGRY

VIOLET.

WHEN CAN WE EAT?

AUNTIE.

I'VE HAD ENOUGH
OF YOUR COMPLAINING
YOU HAVE GOT ME STRAINING
NOT TO SAY SOMETHING PROFANE
AM I SPEAKING IN VAIN,
OR SHOULD I DELIVER
SOME BRUISES OR A WELT
WITH THE BUCKLE ON YOUR AUNTIE'S BELT?

DAISY & VIOLET. No!!!

AUNTIE.

WOULD YOU RATHER
I TOOK A BUTCHER KNIFE
AND CUT YOU APART
SO YOU'D HAVE A NORMAL LIFE?

Good. Not another peep. We're going to see some doctors.

(**AUNTIE** *grabs them roughly and pushes them ahead of her.* **FOUR DOCTORS** *appear.*)

DOCTOR #1.
>IN THE NAME OF MEDICAL ADVANCEMENT
>SURGERY WILL BE AN ENHANCEMENT
>AND GIVE THEM LIVES OF THEIR OWN

DOCTOR #2.
>LIVES OF THEIR OWN

DOCTOR #1.
>LIVES OF THEIR OWN

DOCTOR #3.
>WE'LL CUT INTO SKIN
>THEN THROUGH SUB-DERMAL FLESH

DOCTOR #2.
>ONLY A LITTLE FLESH

DOCTOR #4.
>CUT THROUGH THAT BIT OF FLESH

DOCTOR #1.
>WHEN THEY ARE SEP'RATE
>AND THEY NO LONGER MESH
>YOU'LL THANK US FROM
>THE BOTTOM OF YOUR HEART
>IF YOU LET US CUT THEM APART

ALL DOCTORS.
>CUT, CUT THEM APART

>>*(As **DOCTORS** take **AUNTIE** to one side and haggle over contractual terms, the **TWINS** sing.)*

DAISY & VIOLET.
>I WILL NEVER LEAVE YOU

ALL DOCTORS.
>MADAME, SIGN
>RIGHT HERE ON THIS LINE

DAISY & VIOLET.	**DOCTORS.**
I WILL NEVER GO AWAY	YOUR TWINS WILL BE FINE
WE WERE MEANT TO SHARE	
EACH MOMENT	
	WHY NOT SIGN?
NO MATTER WHAT	
OTHERS MAY SAY	DON'T DECLINE
	HERE'S THE LINE SIGN

DAISY & VIOLET.
> SEEMS LIKE EV'RYBODY
> WANTS TO SPLIT US IN TWO

ALL DOCTORS.
> JOIN OUR GRAND DESIGN

DAISY & VIOLET.
> BUT I WILL NEVER LEAVE YOU

DOCTORS.
> MADAME, SIGN

AUNTIE.
> I AM BUT A POOR WOMAN
> ALL ALONE
> THEY'RE THE ONLY THING OF VALUE
> THAT I OWN
> OTHER DOCTORS HAVE INFORMED US
> ONE OR BOTH COULD DIE FROM SEPARATION
> I WOULD NEED SOME COMPENSATION!

> > *(The* **DOCTORS** *shake their heads "no."* **AUNTIE** *glares at the twins, then exits angrily.)*

VIOLET. Auntie put us back on display…with our clothes off…

DAISY. …In the back room of a pub. People paid money.

VIOLET. They came from everywhere…

DAISY. …Including men in the show business who started…

DAISY & VIOLET. …Booking us in circuses.

VIOLET. It was awful.

DAISY. But sometimes wonderful too. Some of the people we met…

VIOLET. …Including one magical man…

DAISY. …Who crossed the ocean to see us…

DAISY & VIOLET. …The great Houdini!

> > *(***HOUDINI** *is seen in silhouette, hanging upside down in a straight jacket. He wriggles free, magically appearing on stage.)*

DAISY. He taught us something…

VIOLET. …That would change our lives forever.

HOUDINI. Oh my. Aren't you beautiful.

DAISY. Us?

HOUDINI. Yes, you. And you. Phenomenal. Gorgeous!

VIOLET. Most people think we're strange.

HOUDINI. What's wrong with that?

DAISY. Mr. Houdini, you're a magician…

HOUDINI. Escapologist.

VIOLET. Even better. Teach me how to escape from her!

HOUDINI. Sure. Are you ready?

VIOLET. I was joking.

HOUDINI. No you weren't.

[MUSIC. NO. 6A: "FLASHBACK (PART 2) – ALL IN THE MIND."]

[YOU CAN] ALWAYS BE ALONE
FIND A SPACE THAT'S ALL YOUR OWN
IF YOU NEED TO
TAP RESOURCES DEEP WITHIN
TO ESCAPE THE CLANG AND DIN
THAT IMPEDE YOU

IT'S ALL IN THE MIND
THE SHACKLES AND CHAINS
THE DOUBTS THAT CAN BLIND
THE FEAR THAT CONSTRAINS
THE FREEDOM TO FLOAT
TO LIVE UNCONFINED
IT'S ALL IN THE MIND

DAISY. But she's always right here!

HOUDINI.

SO YOU CLOSE A DOOR INSIDE AND HIDE

VIOLET. Hide?

HOUDINI.

IN A SECRET PLACE YOU'LL FIND
WHERE YOU'RE FREE AND UNENTWINED

DAISY. But how?

HOUDINI.

HAVEN'T YOU EVER BEEN IN CONVERSATION
AND YOUR MIND DRIFTED SOMEWHERE ELSE?
OR BEEN IN A ROOM SURROUNDED BY PEOPLE
AND YET FELT A MILLION MILES AWAY?

DAISY.

OH YES, I HAVE

VIOLET. Of course.

HOUDINI.

WELL THAT'S WHERE TO GO
WHEN YOU WANT TO BE ALONE
YOU CAN GO THERE RIGHT NOW
IF YOU REALLY WANT TO

DAISY & VIOLET.

WE CAN'T DISAPPEAR LIKE YOU

HOUDINI.

That's not true.

YOU CAN GO, BUT I'LL RETURN
WITH SOME PRACTICE YOU WILL LEARN
SEPARATING
WHEN YOU MENTALLY ARE FREE
YOU CAN COME AND VISIT ME
I'LL BE WAITING

IT'S ALL IN THE MIND
THE JOY AND THE DREAD
THE WAY WE'RE DEFINED
THE LIES WE'VE BEEN FED
THE KEY TO ESCAPE RESTRICTIONS THAT BIND
IT'S ALL IN THE MIND
ALL IN THE MIND

> (**HOUDINI** *disappears as magically as he appeared.*)

[MUSIC NO. 6B: "FLASHBACK (PART 3)."]

VIOLET. Then Auntie met a balloon salesman. Myer Myers.

DAISY. She called him Sir.

(**SIR** *is revealed with* **AUNTIE**.)

They were quite a team. As soon as they were married…

VIOLET. Sir decided to…

DAISY & VIOLET. …broaden our horizons.

SIR. The good ole' US of A – always hungry for novelty.

COME SEE A NEW LAND
GREAT RICHES AT HAND
RUBES AND COUNTRY HICKS RIPE FOR FLEECING
OUR WEALTH INCREASING
TO BEAT THE BAND
I HAVE GOT IT ALL PLANNED
COME SEE A NEW LAND

VIOLET. We were so excited to come to America…

DAISY. …But Auntie and Sir worked us harder than ever and then…

VIOLET. Auntie started failing.

(**AUNTIE** *fans herself.*)

DAISY. And she died.

(**AUNTIE** *falls backwards.* **SIR** *catches her.*)

Before the body was even cold…

VIOLET. …Sir petitioned the court for custody…

DAISY. …Even though we were legally of age.

(**SIR** *drops* **AUNTIE**. *Pleads to a* **JUDGE**.)

SIR. Thank you, Your Honor.

WON'T YOU PLEASE FORGIVE ME
IF I SEEM EMOTIONAL
FOR THESE POOR DEFORMED GIRLS?
THEY'RE INCAPABLE OF A LIFE ON THEIR OWN
DISABLED FROM BIRTH
THEY NEED A FULL-TIME GUARDIAN
TO ASSIST THEM DAY AND NIGHT
THOUGH NOW I'VE LOST MY BETTER HALF
I AM WILLING TO DO WHAT'S RIGHT

DAISY. The court made us Sir's property…

VIOLET. …His to do with as he pleased…

DAISY. …Completely under his control…

DAISY & VIOLET. …For the rest of our lives.

> *(They sing in counterpoint with the characters they've just described. The* **ENSEMBLE** *underscores with "Ahs.")*

I WILL NEVER LEAVE YOU

HOUDINI.

IT'S ALL IN THE MIND

SIR.

YOU WILL NEVER LEAVE ME

AUNTIE.

LOOK AT YOU GIRLS

DO AS I SAY

JUDGE.

YOU WILL NEVER LEAVE HIM

SIR.

YOU WILL NEVER LEAVE ME

DAISY & VIOLET.

I WILL NEVER LEAVE YOU

AUNTIE.

YOU SHOULD THANK ME EV'RY DAY

DOCTORS.	**JUDGE, DAISY, VIOLET, SIR**.	**HOUDINI**.
CUT, CUT THEM APART, CUT, CUT THEM APART, CUT, CUT, THEM APART	I [YOU] WILL NEVER LEAVE YOU [ME] [HIM]	IT'S ALL IN THE MIND

> *(The characters from the past fade away revealing* **BUDDY** *and* **TERRY** *as at the start of flashback.)*

TERRY. Thank you. Thank you for trusting us with your story.

VIOLET. It's shameful.

BUDDY. No. It's inspiring. Look at all you've survived.

DAISY. It feels good to finally tell someone.

TERRY. You need to tell it to a court.

VIOLET. I could never do that.

BUDDY. Don't worry, Violet. You've got truth on your side.

TERRY. And me. Once I get your story out there, every man in this country will want to defend you and every woman will want to be your friend.

VIOLET. You have a high opinion of yourself.

TERRY. I have a high opinion of you! Buddy!

> *(MUSIC NO. 6C: "BEFORE THE TRIAL.")*

> (**BUDDY** *goes off.*)

Now Daisy, you've always wanted to be onstage. Just think of testifying as another performance. Most trials are won or lost before anyone even steps foot in the courtroom. First we have to get you looking beautiful. New hairstyles, make-up, dresses…

> (**BUDDY** *returns with a costume rack.*)

Not those dresses. Less Jean Harlow. More Mary Pickford.

> (**BUDDY** *pops a pair of demure hats on the twins' heads.*)

Next we need to find a reporter who'll present your story in the most sympathetic light.

TERRY. *(As* **REPORTER**.*)* If you win your freedom, what do you intend to do?

VIOLET. Have a cocktail.

DAISY. Have a man.

TERRY. No. Buddy, let's show 'em.

> *(As* **LAWYER**.*)*

If you win your freedom, what do you intend to do?

BUDDY. *(As* **DAISY**.*)* Earn a living.

TERRY. Then?

BUDDY. *(As* **VIOLET**.*)* Share it.

TERRY. With who?

BUDDY. Orphans.

DAISY. *(Getting the idea.)* And people with disabilities greater than our own.

TERRY. Good! Now onto the testimony. We'll find a great lawyer, someone charming, handsome, sophisticated…

> *(He decides to play the* **LAWYER**.*)*

Did Sir ever beat you?

BUDDY. *(As* **DAISY**.*)* Yes he did

> *(As* **VIOLET**.*)*

Sometimes with the buckle of his belt.

TERRY. How many hours a day does he make you work?

BUDDY. *(As* **DAISY**.*)* Sixteen! Sixteen!

> *(As* **VIOLET**.*)*

Seven days a week.

TERRY. Even on Sundays! And what does he pay you for all that work?

BUDDY. *(As* **VIOLET**.*)* Not one thin dime.

TERRY. *(Jumping out of character.)* Wait… Is that really true?

> *(The* **TWINS** *nod.)*

This is going to be easier than I thought.

> *(He takes their hands.)*

Do you trust me?

DAISY. Yes!

> *(***VIOLET** *shoots her a look.)*

TERRY. Great. We've got a lot of work to do, so let's get started.

> *(***BUDDY** *leads them off as the set shifts to a courtroom.)*

TERRY. *(Cont.)*
> THOSE TWO HAVE FACED SO MANY TRIALS
> I'VE FACED A FEW OF MY OWN
> NOW OUR FATES ARE LINKED
> 'CAUSE I HAD A HUNCH
> WHEN I PASSED THAT SIDE SHOW
> THE WHOLE DAMN COUNTRY'S
> ON THE EDGE OF ITS SEAT
> 'CAUSE THE TRIAL OF THE CENTURY'S
> ABOUT TO BEGIN
> AND WHO THE HELL KNOWS
> WE JUST MIGHT WIN

> *(**BUDDY** enters with **DAISY** and **VIOLET**, now dressed for court.)*

BUDDY. I think they're ready.

TERRY. Buddy, they're more than ready…they're perfect. Now you girls have nothing to worry about. Just remember what we told you.

> *(**TERRY** impulsively kisses **DAISY** on the cheek and exits.)*

BUDDY. See you inside.

> *(He nods to **VIOLET** and exits.)*

> *(MUSIC NO. 7: "FEELINGS YOU'VE GOT TO HIDE.")*

DAISY.
> WHY DO I FEEL
> LIKE I SWALLOWED A BUTTERFLY?
> TICK'LING INSIDE
> MAKES ME LAUGH
> TILL I WANT TO CRY
> WHY ARE MY EYES TURNING MOIST
> WHILE MY THROAT IS DRY?
> IS IT THAT SPECIAL GUY?

> WHY ARE MY FEELINGS
> RACING AROUND INSIDE?

WILL I EXPLODE
IF ALL OF MY THOUGHTS COLLIDE?
ONE MINUTE BRAVE
THE NEXT MINUTE TERRIFIED

VIOLET.

THOSE ARE FEELINGS
YOU HAVE GOT TO HIDE

DAISY.

I CAN'T HIDE WHAT I FEEL
THE WAY THAT YOU DO

VIOLET.

WHAT DO YOU MEAN?
THAT I DON'T FLIRT LIKE YOU?

DAISY.

BUDDY'S YOUR DREAM
THE APPLE OF YOUR EYE

VIOLET.

WHY DO YOU SAY THAT?
TELL ME WHY?

DAISY.

I'M YOUR SISTER
I'M YOUR SHADOW
I DO KNOW

VIOLET.

OH YOU KNOW...?

DAISY.

YES I KNOW

VIOLET.

WHAT I'M THINKING

DAISY.

WHAT YOU'RE THINKING
I'M NOT DEAF
I'M NOT BLIND

VIOLET.

YOU CAN ALWAYS

DAISY.	VIOLET.
READ YOUR MIND	READ MY MIND

VIOLET.
  NOW I'M THE ONE
  LIGHTNING UP LIKE A FIREFLY
  NOW I'M THE ONE
  BLUSHING RED
  KISSING PRIDE GOOD-BYE
  WHY DO I WANT TO TELL ALL
  AND YET FEEL SO SHY
  IS IT THAT SPECIAL GUY?

DAISY.
  YOU WANT YOUR BUDDY.
  STANDING THERE BY YOUR SIDE

VIOLET.
  HEART IN MY THROAT
  LIKE I'M ON A MID-WAY RIDE
  BUT I'LL NEVER SHOW
  WHAT'S GOING ON INSIDE
  THESE ARE FEELINGS I'VE GOT TO HIDE

DAISY.
  WHY DO YOU FEEL THAT WAY?

VIOLET.
  FEELINGS AREN'T FOR DISPLAY

DAISY.
  TELL HIM WITHOUT DELAY

VIOLET.
  YOU WOULD SHOUT
  WHAT I WOULD NEVER SAY

    (Direct segue.)

Scene 5
The Courtroom

DAISY.
 WHY ARE MY FEELINGS
 RACING AROUND INSIDE?

VIOLET.
 THESE LONGINGS CAN'T BE SATISFIED

DAISY.
 WILL ALL MY THOUGHTS
  COLLIDE?

 HE LOOKS AT ME WITH
  PRIDE

 ARE THESE
 FEELINGS I'VE GOT TO
  HIDE?

VIOLET.
 THIS WAVE WILL WASH OUT
 WITH THE TIDE

 THESE ARE FEELINGS
 YOU'VE GOT TO HIDE

 FEELINGS I'VE GOT TO
  HIDE?

(Lights change. **DAISY** *and* **VIOLET** *now on the witness stand.)*

[MUSIC NO. 8: "THE COURTROOM."]

SIR'S LAWYER. You testified that Mr. Myers beat you. Did he hit you on your faces?

DAISY & VIOLET. No.

SIR'S LAWYER. On your hands, your arms, your legs?

VIOLET. No, only ever on our backs.

SIR'S LAWYER. As you would discipline any child. And you say he never paid you for your work?

DAISY. That's right.

SIR'S LAWYER. But what about all the money he's been putting aside since you were children? The trust fund that will support you long after Mr. Myers is gone?

VIOLET.
 He never told us about
 that!

DAISY.
 We never knew—

SIR'S LAWYER. Well you do now. This man has clothed you, provided food and shelter, and protected you from danger all these years and now you're asking the court to cast him aside?

(The **TWINS** *have no response.)*

We have no further questions.

(The **TWINS** *leave the witness stand.* **TERRY** *and* **BUDDY** *watch, depressed.)*

BUDDY. Not exactly the way we rehearsed it.

TERRY. Nope.

SIR'S LAWYER. Your Honor, we would like to present one final witness.

(A sense of surprise and anticipation as **JAKE** *enters.)*

VIOLET. Jake?

(He ignores her, moves past the twins to the witness stand.)

SIR'S LAWYER. I would like to thank you for volunteering to appear here today. As a trusted employee of Mr. Myers, you are uniquely qualified to shed light on these outrageous charges against him. You have been with the sideshow for quite some time, isn't that right?

JAKE. Yes, sir.

SIR'S LAWYER. And you were specifically hired to watch after these unfortunate girls?

JAKE. Yes, sir.

SIR'S LAWYER. And that protection included teaching them the difference between right and wrong?

JAKE. Yes, sir.

SIR'S LAWYER. Sometimes when it was necessary, Sir – Mr. Myers – would teach them by giving them the strap, is that not correct?

JAKE. Yes, sir.

SIR'S LAWYER. Have you ever struck someone to help them learn the difference between right and wrong?

JAKE. Yes, sir.

SIR'S LAWYER. So you agree that this man is innocent of the charge of abuse?

JAKE. I've seen many things in my life. I can't rightly say why any human being ought to be treated like somebody's property. I watched this man abuse these girls for ten years.

SIR. What are you doing?

JAKE. What you hired me to do. Protect the girls.

> (**SIR** *lunges toward* **JAKE**. *His* **LAWYER** *restrains him.*)

SIR. You traitor!

JUDGE. Order! Order!

JAKE. Everything they said is true.

SIR'S LAWYER. Your Honor, we ask for an adjournment!

JUDGE. Counsel will convene in my chambers at once.

> (*The* **JUDGE** *knocks the gavel. Court is adjourned.* **TERRY** *and* **BUDDY** *exit toward the* **JUDGE**'s *chambers.* **JAKE** *exits. The* **TWINS** *look heartbroken.* **TERRY** *and* **BUDDY** *rush in.*)

TERRY. *(To* **BUDDY**.*)* You want to tell them?

BUDDY. No you do it –

TERRY. No, you!

> (*Then together…*)

BUDDY.	TERRY.
We won!	You're free!

DAISY. We're free?!

VIOLET. Free.

Scene 6
Sideshow Tent

(The **ATTRACTIONS** *enter and congratulate* **DAISY**
& **VIOLET.***)*

(Music. **SIR** *enters and everyone falls silent.)*

SIR. Ladies and gentlemen, there they are, direct from
their triumph in court. You girls painted me as quite
the ogre. But your fabricated stories can't compare
with the truth I've learned about your friend here.

TERRY. Why be a sore loser? Let's shake hands and go our
separate ways.

SIR. I don't shake hands with liars.

TERRY. What are you talking about?

SIR. I've got friends too. I've done some asking around.
Mr. Connor hasn't worked for the Orpheum Circuit for
a couple of years now.

TERRY. *(To* **SIR***.)* You need better sources. I just signed a
new deal with the Circuit yesterday and the first act
I booked was the Hilton Sisters.

VIOLET. But you told us you already worked for them.

DAISY. So he lied a little. Doesn't everybody in show
business? Violet, he may not be perfect, but he's a lot
better than what we've had.

*(**VIOLET** hesitates, nods. **TERRY** squeezes **DAISY***'s*
hand.)

SIR. Go ahead. Cast your lot with this scum. Good luck to
you.

(Seeing **JAKE** *enter.)*

What are you doing here?

JAKE. Just came to get my things.

SIR. I should have known better than to trust your kind.

(To **ATTRACTIONS***.)*

Time for us to move on. Clearly, this well has been poisoned. We leave at dawn – unless any of you has a better offer?

    (To **DAISY & VIOLET.***)*

As for you ingrates, you'll find out soon enough just what I've been protecting you from.

    (Exits.)

    [MUSIC NO. 9: "SAY GOODBYE TO THE SIDESHOW."]

VIOLET.

WHAT HAVE WE DONE?

DAISY.

LOST OUR HOMES

VIOLET.

CLOSED A DOOR

TERRY.

OPENED MORE!

SAY GOODBYE TO THE SIDESHOW
TO THE DEBTS YOU WERE TOLD YOU OWE
NOW YOU'RE FIN'LLY FREE TO GO
SAY GOODBYE TO THE SIDESHOW

ATTRACTIONS.

GOODBYE

DAISY

GOODBYE, WE WILL MISS YOU

HALF MAN/HALF WOMAN.

DON'T CRY, LET ME KISS YOU

VIOLET.

OH MY
WHY SHOULD IT BE SO HARD
TO SAY GOODBYE?

VENUS DE MILO.

FAREWELL, DON'T FORGET US

BEARDED LADY.

    DO TELL HOW YOU MET US

DOG BOY.

    STAY STRONG WHEN PEOPLE TREAT YOU WRONG

LIZARD MAN.

    FAREWELL, SO LONG

FORTUNE TELLER.

    NOW, NOW

    SAYING GOODBYE IS PART OF GROWING UP

    THERE'S A WHOLE NEW WORLD

    OF FRIENDS FOR YOU TO MAKE

JAKE.

    GOODBYE, DAISY

    DEAR, SWEET VIOLET.

DAISY & VIOLET.

    OH NO, NOT GOOD-BYE TO JAKE

JAKE.

    TAKE WING, FLY TO GLORY

    DANCE, SING, TELL YOUR STORY

    YOU BRING SUCH JOY

    TO THOSE YOU'VE KNOWN

    TAKE FLIGHT, TAKE WING

TERRY.

    JAKE, LOOKS LIKE THEIR HEARTS MIGHT BREAK

    SAYING GOODBYE TO YOU

    WE COULD USE YOU BACKSTAGE

    AS WE TOUR WITH THEIR SHOW

    NOTHING FOR YOU HERE

    SO WHY NOT GO?

DAISY.

    YES, SAY YES

VIOLET.

    PLEASE COME ALONG

JAKE.

    NOTHING LOST IF I DECIDE TO

    I FEEL I BELONG BESIDE YOU

ATTRACTIONS.

SAY GOODBYE TO THE SIDESHOW
WE'LL BE CHEERING YOU AS YOU GO
WE ALWAYS KNEW YOU WOULD OUTGROW
THE TENTS OF THE SIDESHOW
GOODBYE

> (**DAISY** *and* **VIOLET** *wave goodbye to the* **ATTRACTIONS** *as* **TERRY** *and* **BUDDY** *lead them offstage.*)

MALE ATTRACTIONS.

STRIKE TENTS

ATTRACTIONS.

PULL THE STAKES UP
GO GENTS
LET THE BRAKES UP
NO FENCE
STOPS US FROM MOVING ON
TO OUR NEXT SHOW
SO LONG

FEMALE ATTRACTIONS.

WE ADORE YOU

ATTRACTIONS.

WE'LL BE
ROOTING FOR YOU
STAY STRONG WHEN PEOPLE TREAT YOU WELL

GROUP 1.

FAREWELL

GROUP 2.

SO LONG

> (**JAKE** *enters with suitcase.*)

ATTRACTIONS.

GOODBYE

> (**JAKE** *runs off. Musical segue as set changes.*)

Scene 7
Vaudeville

(The Hilton sisters' debut.)

ANNOUNCER. Ladies and gentlemen… Chicago's Orpheum theatre is proud to present the debut of the greatest double act the world has ever seen… Daisy and Violet Hilton!

(**SUITORS** *enter, dance and sing.)*

[MUSIC NO. 11: "READY TO PLAY."]

SUITORS.

ARE YOU READY?
FOR WHAT THIS DUO CAN DO?
ARE YOU READY?
TO SEE THIS DAZZLING DEBUT?
ARE YOU READY
TO CHASE YOUR BLUES AWAY?
WE'RE SO READY
THEY'RE SO READY
WE ARE READY TO PLAY!

(The **SUITORS** *underscore* **DAISY** *and* **VIOLET** *throughout song.)*

DAISY & VIOLET.

I'M SO TIRED OF BEING WEALTHY
WHY CAN'T I BE POOR BUT HEALTHY?
BORED AND RICH IS SO PASSÉ
AND NOW I'M READY TO PLAY

SUITORS.

YEAH!

DAISY & VIOLET.

DADDY'S DOWN AT THE CASINO
MUMMY'S OUT WITH VALENTINO
GAVE THE STAFF A HOLIDAY
AND NOW I'M READY TO PLAY

CALLED ALL THE HANDSOME GUYS
I KNOW

INVITED THEM OUT TO MY CHATEAU
HOPE I FIND MY ROMEO

ALL.

'CAUSE I AM READY TO GO, GO, GO!

DAISY & VIOLET.

GOT THE URGE

SUITORS.

GOT THE URGE

DAISY & VIOLET.

TO MIX AND MINGLE
WHY NOT MERGE

SUITORS.

WHY NOT MERGE

DAISY & VIOLET.

WITH LIPS A-TINGLE?

SUITORS.

MWAH!

DAISY & VIOLET.

ALL ALONE SINCE NOON TODAY

SUITORS.

HEY

ALL.

AND NOW I'M READY
OH SO READY
NOW I'M READY TO PLAY!

SUITORS.

THEY'VE GOT CHIC GOWNS
THEY'RE SABLE-STOLED
RUBIES, DIAMONDS

DAISY & VIOLET.

LOTS OF GOLD

SUITORS.

GOLD!

DAISY & VIOLET.

ALL THAT FLASH
GETS IN MY WAY

SUITORS.

WHEN THEY GET READY TO PLAY

ALL.

LET'S PLAY!

(Dance break.)

DAISY & VIOLET.

HUNDREDS OF BOYFRIENDS
AREN'T ENOUGH

SUITORS.

UNH UNH

DAISY & VIOLET.

I'M NOT A WISPY POWDER PUFF

SUITORS.

NO!

DAISY & VIOLET.

I LIKE MY JAZZ A LITTLE ROUGH

ALL.

'CAUSE I AM READY
TO STRUT MY STUFF!

DAISY & VIOLET.

I WOULD LIKE

SUITORS.

OH YEAH!

DAISY & VIOLET.

A SIMPLE ROMANCE
MAJOR HOLDINGS

SUITORS.

UH HUH!

DAISY & VIOLET.

AND MINOR REMBRANDTS
IF HE'S CUTE I'LL LET HIM PAY

ALL.

'CAUSE NOW I'M READY
OH SO READY

DAISY & VIOLET.

NOW I'M READY

DAISY.

TO PLAY!

VIOLET.

LET'S PLAY

ALL.

LET'S PLAY!

(Musical segue as set changes.)

Scene 8
Backstage

[MUSIC NO. 11A: "AFTER THE SHOW."]

(**BUDDY** *and* **JAKE** *enter excitedly.*)

BUDDY. Jake, did you see what's going on out there? There must be a thousand people lined up at the stage door just to get a look at the girls –

JAKE. Sure beats the crowd at the side show.

(**TERRY** *enters excitedly.*)

TERRY. Gentlemen, we did it!

BUDDY. Well, they did it.

TERRY. Yes, they did it. But we're a team. Jake, I you take such good care of our girls. And, Buddy, I always knew you were the guy to turn them into stars.

(**DAISY** *and* **VIOLET** *enter.*)

Magnificent!

(*He kisses* **DAISY**.)

BUDDY. Wonderful!

VIOLET. I actually enjoyed myself.

BUDDY. Oh, Violet, that makes me so happy…

(*Kisses* **VIOLET**.)

DAISY. If we always get kisses, we'll try even harder.

TERRY. Kisses are a tiny reward.

VIOLET. Not for us.

BUDDY. Then get ready for another.

TERRY. And another.

(**DAISY** *holds on to the kiss.* **TERRY** *doesn't fight her.*)

BUDDY. And just one more.

(**REPORTERS** *enter.* **TERRY** *presents his clients.*)

TERRY. Ladies and gentlemen, the Hilton Sisters!

[MUSIC NO. 11B: "THE INTERVIEW."]

REPORTER #5.

WE'VE GOT A MILLION QUESTIONS FOR YOU

REPORTER #8.

COULD YOU BE SEPARATED?

REPORTER #6.

HAVE DOCTORS EXAMINED YOU?

DAISY.

IN HUNDREDS OF WAYS

VIOLET.

FROM OUR EARLIEST DAYS

DAISY.

SOME SAY WE COULD BE SEPARATED

VIOLET.

SOME WOULD LOVE TO TRY

DAISY & VIOLET.

SOME SAY WE WOULD DIE

REPORTER #1.

WHAT ABOUT ROMANCE?

REPORTER #5.

WHAT ABOUT LOVE?

REPORTER #6.

WHAT ABOUT BEAUS?

VIOLET.

OH THOSE

I SUPPOSE

IT'S BOUND TO HAPPEN

DAISY.

SOME DAY

VIOLET.

SOME NIGHT

WHEN THE MOON

IS JUST RIGHT

DAISY.

WHEN THE UNIVERSE HUMS

VIOLET.

> WHEN THE GUY COMES ALONG
> WHO HEARS THE SINGER
> MORE THAN THE SONG

DAISY.

> SOME DAY

VIOLET.

> SOME NIGHT

DAISY & VIOLET.

> LOVE WILL FEEL RIGHT

> > *(Lights change to indicate the* **TWINS**' *inner thoughts.)*

VIOLET.

> BUDDY KISSED ME
> HE KISSED ME
> FOR THE FIRST TIME

DAISY.

> A LITTLE KISS
> TO SAY "GOOD SHOW"
> I WANT MORE KISSES TO FOLLOW

VIOLET.

> YOUR LIPS PROVE WE'RE SHARING
> THE WARMTH THAT I FELT
> THE FROST ON MY HEART
> IS BEGINNING TO MELT

DAISY.

> YOU CAN'T MINIMIZE
> THE HEAT IN YOUR EYES
> YOUR PASSION IS NOT A SURPRISE

> > *(Light change to* **DAISY** *and* **VIOLET** *back in real time.)*

REPORTER #6.

> YOU'RE WORKING WITH SEVERAL MEN.

REPORTER #7.

> LIKE TERRY.

REPORTER #9.

THAT FOSTER KID.

REPORTER #6.

THE COLORED BOY?

REPORTER #4.

HOW CLOSE ARE ALL OF YOU?

REPORTER #8.

VERY CLOSE?

VIOLET.

WE WOULDN'T BE HERE WITHOUT THEIR HELP

DAISY.

WE SHARE THE APPLAUSE WITH THEM

REPORTER #6.

ANYTHING ELSE?

REPORTER #1.

YOUR ROOM?

REPORTER #6.

YOUR BED?

JAKE. Watch your mouth, Mister!

TERRY. Jake, I'll handle this.

> *(To* **REPORTERS**.*)*

Not to throw cold water on your sick fantasizing, but this is strictly business. No romance involved. I have a girl of my own.

REPORTER #9. A girl?

REPORTER #4. You always have more than one.

BUDDY. We'd never take advantage of the twins. We don't think of them that way.

REPORTER 5. *(To a* **COLLEAGUE.***)* Of course he doesn't. They're girls.

> *(Lights change to* **DAISY** *and* **VIOLET***'s inner thoughts.)*

DAISY.

> I'M NOT REALLY HERE
> NOTHING THEY'RE SAYING
> IS CATCHING MY EAR

VIOLET.

> AND I'M VIRTUALLY BLIND
> NO MORE ROOM IN MY MIND
> HE KISSED ME

DAISY.

> ONE MINUTE BLISS
> BECAUSE OF HIS KISS
> THEN CRIPPLING DOUBT
> WHEN THE TRUTH COMES OUT
> ALL THAT I FELT WAS A LIE

VIOLET.

> I FELT LOVE WITHIN YOU

DAISY.

> HOW CAN WE CONTINUE?

VIOLET.

> THE SEEDS WE HAVE PLANTED
> WILL BLOOM

DAISY.

> ENOUGH OF THESE QUESTIONS

VIOLET.

> I CAN'T HEAR THE QUESTIONS

DAISY & VIOLET.

> I CAN'T KEEP MY MIND IN THE ROOM
>
> *(Lights change to* **DAISY** *and* **VIOLET** *back in real time.)*

REPORTER 6.

> DON'T YOU NEED A MAN?

REPORTER 3.

> DON'T YOU WANT TO GET MARRIED?

REPORTER 1.

HUSBANDS?

REPORTERS 2, 6 & 7.

CHILDREN?

REPORTERS 3, 4, 5, 7, 8, 9 & 10.

FAMILIES?

VIOLET.

LIKE ANY GIRLS OUR AGE
WE DREAM OF GETTING MARRIED
A WEDDING

DAISY.

A HUSBAND

VIOLET.

A FAM'LY TO COME HOME TO

REPORTERS 1, 2, 3, 4, 8 & 9.

HOW WOULD THAT WORK?

REPORTERS 5, 6, 7 & 10.

HOW WOULD THAT WORK?

ALL REPORTERS.

WITH YOUR CONDITION?

DAISY.

ANYTHING'S POSSIBLE

VIOLET.

WHEN EV'RYTHING'S RIGHT

DAISY.

I'M DAISY.

VIOLET.

I'M VIOLET.

TERRY.

GOOD NIGHT.

> (**JAKE** *and* **TERRY** *usher the grumbling* **REPORTERS** *Off.* **BUDDY** *looks sadly at* **VIOLET**, *then exits.*)

[MUSIC NO. 11C: "BUDDY KISSED ME."]

VIOLET.
> BUDDY
> KISSED ME
> HE KISSED ME FOR THE FIRST TIME

DAISY.
> DIDN'T YOU HEAR WHAT HE SAID?

VIOLET.
> THERE'S ONLY ONE THOUGHT
> RUNNING THROUGH MY HEAD
> HE KISSED ME

DAISY.
> AND THEN THEY BOTH DENIED
> ANY THOUGHT OF ROMANCE

VIOLET.
> BUT HE KISSED ME
> WORDS CAN LIE
> BUT KISSES DON'T

DAISY.
> YOU CAN LIE TO YOURSELF
> I WON'T
> NO ONE COULD LOVE A SIAMESE TWIN
> NOBODY WANTS US
> NO ONE EVER HAS
> NO ONE EVER WILL

VIOLET.
> WHY ARE YOU TRYING TO KILL MY DREAM?

DAISY.
> IT'S NOT A DREAM
> IT'S A NIGHTMARE
> WAKE UP
> LOOK AROUND YOU
> WE ARE FREAKS
> STUCK TOGETHER
> AND WE'LL ALWAYS BE ALONE

VIOLET.

    BUT I WANT TO WAKE UP
    TO WHAT I'M DREAMING OF
    DREAMING THAT SOMEDAY
    SOME NIGHT
    I COULD FIND LOVE
    WILL I FIND LOVE?

      [MUSIC NO. 12: "WHO WILL LOVE ME AS I AM?"]

VIOLET.

    LIKE A FISH PLUCKED FROM THE OCEAN
    TOSSED INTO A FOREIGN STREAM
    ALWAYS KNEW THAT I WAS DIFFERENT
    OFTEN FLED INTO A DREAM
    I IGNORED THE RAGING CURRENTS
    RIGHT AGAINST THE TIDE I SWAM
    BUT I FLOATED WITH THE QUESTION
    WHO WILL LOVE ME AS I AM?

DAISY.

    LIKE AN ODD EXOTIC CREATURE
    ON DISPLAY INSIDE A ZOO
    HEARING CHILDREN ASKING QUESTIONS
    MAKES ME ASK SOME QUESTIONS TOO
    COULD WE BEND THE LAWS OF NATURE?
    COULD A LION LOVE A LAMB?
    WHO COULD SEE BEYOND THIS SURFACE?
    WHO WILL LOVE ME AS I AM?

DAISY & VIOLET.

    WHO WILL EVER CALL
    TO SAY I LOVE YOU?
    SEND ME FLOWERS OR A TELEGRAM?
    WHO COULD PROUDLY STAND BESIDE ME?
    WHO WILL LOVE ME AS I AM?

DAISY.

    LIKE A CLOWN WHOSE TEARS CAUSE LAUGHTER
    TRAPPED BEHIND A PAINTED MASK

VIOLET.
> EVEN SEEING SMILING FACES
> I STILL FEEL I HAVE TO ASK

DAISY & VIOLET.
> WHO WOULD WANT TO JOIN THIS MADNESS?
> WHO WOULD CHANGE MY MONOGRAM?
> WHO WILL BE PART OF MY CIRCUS?
> WHO WILL LOVE ME AS I AM?

> WHO WILL EVER CALL TO SAY I LOVE YOU?
> SEND ME FLOWERS OR A TELEGRAM?
> WHO COULD PROUDLY STAND BESIDE ME?
> WHO WILL LOVE ME AS I AM?

> *(The* **ATTRACTIONS** *are revealed.)*

ENSEMBLE.
> WHO COULD PROUDLY STAND BESIDE ME

ALL.
> WHO WILL LOVE ME AS I AM?

End of Act I.

ACT II

[MUSIC NO. 13: "ENTR'ACTE."]

Scene 1
Onstage/Backstage At The Palace

*(***DAISY*** *and* **VIOLET** *enter.* **BUDDY** *enters stage left, crosses to* **VIOLET** *and falls to one knee.)*

[MUSIC NO. 14: "STUCK WITH YOU (PART 1)."]

BUDDY.

MARRY ME, VIOLET

*(Another suitor – ***RAY***, dressed to match* **BUDDY**, *enters stage right, crosses to* **DAISY** *and falls to one knee.)*

RAY.

MARRY ME, DAISY

RAY AND BUDDY.

MAKE ME HAPPY

THE REST OF MY LIFE

RAY.

MARRY ME, DAISY

BUDDY.

MARRY ME, VIOLET

BUDDY AND RAY.

WHY CAN'T WE BE

HUSBAND AND WIFE?

DAISY & VIOLET.
> I WARNED YOU
> ABOUT MY CIRCUMSTANCES
> HOW OLD ROMANCES
> FELL THROUGH

>> *(A drop is revealed depicting the entrance to a romanticized manufacturing plant. Across the top of the gate is a sign reading "Dad's Glue Factory.")*

> DAD'S BUS'NESS CAUSED MY LOVE LIFE
> TO BE FRACTURED
> HE MANUFACTURED
> STRONG GLUE

DAISY. *(Offering her hand to* **RAY.***)*
> BUT YOU PERSISTED ANYWAY

VIOLET. *(Offering her hand to* **BUDDY.***)*
> AND NOW IT SEEMS YOU'RE HERE TO STAY

DAISY & VIOLET.
> DAD'S PRODUCT HAS MADE ONE
> WHERE THERE WERE TWO
> AND NOW I'M

>> *(***DAISY*** and* **VIOLET*** try to withdraw their hands but they're "stuck." During the following the four try to disengage.)*

> STUCK WITH YOU
> OH YES I'M
> STUCK WITH YOU
> GUESS THERE ARE WORSE THINGS TO BE
> 'CAUSE EVEN THOUGH
> WE CAN'T BE SEPARATED
> DISSOCIATED
> OR ISOLATED
> AT LEAST YOU'RE ALSO STUCK WITH…

BUDDY. Stop!

>> *(***RAY***,* **BUDDY***,* **DAISY***,* **VIOLET*** and orchestra stop as the lights change. They are in rehearsal, not performance.)*

Ray, you two need to match what we're doing on this side.

DAISY. Don't listen to him, Ray. You do everything perfectly.

BUDDY. Daisy, I'm trying to polish this number! If you spent half as much time learning the steps as you do flirting...

DAISY. Flirting? You mean like this?

VIOLET. Daisy!

TERRY. *(Entering from the wings.)* What's the matter, Buddy?

BUDDY. Nothing, nothing...a little choreography problem.

TERRY. I told you it was a mistake to put yourself in the number.

BUDDY. I'm working it out!

DAISY. Ray and I can work out our problems in private. Wanna watch, Buddy?

BUDDY. Take five, everyone.

(He exits and **RAY** *runs after him.)*

TERRY. Daisy – there are people around.

DAISY. So?

TERRY. We're selling you and Violet as "typical girls next door."

DAISY. Typical girls have boyfriends. Wann be mine?

*(***TERRY*** glowers at her and exits.)*

[MUSIC NO. 15: "LEAVE ME ALONE."]

VIOLET.
    YOU ARE SHAMELESS
    A SHAMELESS FLIRT

DAISY.
    YOU ARE A BORING INTROVERT

VIOLET.
    WELL, I'M NOT A JEZEBEL

DAISY.

SO YOU'D PREFER I ACT LIKE YOU?
AFRAID OF YOUR FEELINGS
AFRAID THEY'RE TABOO
HOW WILL YOUR BUDDY EVER HAVE A CLUE
THAT YOU LOVE HIM THROUGH AND THROUGH?

VIOLET.

DON'T SAY THAT!
HE MIGHT OVERHEAR

DAISY.

SO WHAT?
WHY LIVE IN FEAR?
HE MIGHT FEEL THE SAME
BUT HE'S SHY

VIOLET.

SO AM I!
I DESPISE
THE WAY YOU ADVERTISE

DAISY.

I HATE YOUR COY LITTLE ACT

VIOLET.

IS THAT A FACT?

DAISY.

LEAVE ME ALONE
THIS IS NONE OF YOUR BUS'NESS
YOU DON'T NEED TO JUDGE
OR OFFER ADVICE

VIOLET.

IF YOU COULD SEE YOU
FROM MY PERSPECTIVE
YOU WOULDN'T LIKE WHAT YOU WERE SHOWN
NO I WON'T LEAVE YOU ALONE

DAISY.

LEAVE ME ALONE

VIOLET.

AND HOW WOULD I DO THAT?

DAISY.

LEAVE ME ALONE

VIOLET.

TELL ME WHERE WOULD I GO?

DAISY.

LEAVE ME ALONE

VIOLET.

BELIEVE ME I'D LOVE TO

DAISY.

I NEED SOME TIME OF MY OWN

DAISY.	**VIOLET.**
LEAVE ME ALONE	LEAVE YOU ALONE?
YOU DON'T KNOW	CAN YOU HEAR
WHAT YOU'RE SAYING	WHAT YOU'RE SAYING?
YOU'LL NEVER FIND LOVE	YOU WON'T FIND LOVE
BY PLAYING IT SHY	BY CHASING THE GUY
DON'T NEED THE WISDOM	IT'S NOT WISDOM
OR THE OPINION	JUST OPINION

DAISY.

YOU GRANDLY DISPENSE

FROM YOUR THRONE

VIOLET.

MY THRONE? OH NO

DAISY.	**VIOLET.**
WHY DON'T YOU LEAVE ME ALONE?	I WON'T LEAVE YOU ALONE

DAISY.

THAT'S WHAT I'M ASKING

VIOLET.

LEAVE YOU ALONE?

DAISY.

IT'S A SIMPLE REQUEST

VIOLET.

LEAVE YOU ALONE?

DAISY.

I'D BE FINE WITHOUT YOU

I NEED SOME TIME ON MY OWN

VIOLET.

I DON'T LIKE YOUR TONE

DAISY.

WHY DON'T YOU

VIOLET.

HOW COULD I

DAISY.

I HATE YOU

VIOLET.

SO DO I

DAISY.	**VIOLET.**
WHY DON'T YOU	WHY WOULD I
LEAVE ME ALONE?	LEAVE YOU ALONE?

(Musical segue back to the number they were previously rehearsing, now in full performance. Their act has obviously grown in stature – bigger sets, fancy costumes.)

[MUSIC NO. 15A: "STUCK WITH YOU (PART 2)."]

DAISY & VIOLET.

STUCK WITH YOU

OH YES I'M

STUCK WITH YOU

DAISY, VIOLET, BUDDY, RAY

GUESS THERE ARE WORSE THINGS TO BE

'CAUSE NOW THAT WE'RE FOREVER AGGREGATED

AMALGAMATED

AFFILIATED

AT LEAST YOU'RE ALSO STUCK WITH ME

*(Dance break, the four moving as one, **ALL** "stuck" together.)*

DAISY.

YOU DIDN'T SEEM

TO BE THE DREAM

THAT I IMAGINED

VIOLET.
I WASN'T SMITTEN AT FIRST

DAISY & VIOLET.
AND IF THE TEST
WAS FOR THE BEST

DAISY.
YOU DIDN'T ACE IT

VIOLET.
BUT LET'S FACE IT

DAISY & VIOLET.
YOU WEREN'T THE WORST

DAISY, VIOLET, BUDDY & RAY.
I GUESS THAT I'M
STUCK WITH YOU
OH YES I'M STUCK WITH YOU

DAISY & VIOLET.
GUESS THERE ARE
WORSE THINGS TO BE

RAY & BUDDY. *(Staggered, overlapping with above.)*
THERE ARE WORSE THINGS TO BE

DAISY, VIOLET, BUDDY & RAY.
'CAUSE EVEN THOUGH
WE CAN'T BE SEPARATED
DISSOCIATED
OR ISOLATED
AT LEAST YOU'RE ALSO
STUCK WITH ME

(Song ends. Musical segue.)

[MUSIC NO. 15B: "STUCK WITH YOU (PLAYOFF)."]

Scene 2
Manhattan Penthouse

[MUSIC NO. 16: "NEW YEAR'S EVE."]

*(**TERRY** greets elegant New Yorkers, dressed to the nines.)*

*(**JAKE** enters, also dressed up. Two **GUESTS** try to give him their empty glasses.)*

TERRY. He's with me.

*(The two **GUESTS** look confused, then retreat.)*

Jake! Looking fine. Some digs, huh?

JAKE. Long way from the sideshow.

TERRY. Let me tell you, success is even sweeter when you've been on the bottom.

JAKE. You think I was always King of the Cannibals? I had to eat my way to the top.

TERRY. I've never asked…where'd Sir find you? Georgia? Louisiana?

JAKE. Hackensack.

TERRY. And look at you now! From that seedy tent to working with the highest paid act in vaudeville.

JAKE. The two places ain't that different. The girls are working just as hard, if not harder.

TERRY. They need to rake it in while they can. I'm looking for a new angle – something to get them to whatever's next – radio. A recording career.

JAKE. *(Baiting him.)* Hell – they could even be movie stars, right?

TERRY. They're pretty enough and Daisy's got the charisma. But I don't think those special effects guys can make a whole person disappear.

*(**JAKE** smiles to himself. **BUDDY** and **RAY** enter.)*

Tell the girls it's time for their entrance.

*(**JAKE** exits.)*

(To **BUDDY**.*)* You and Ray have been spending a lot of time together.

BUDDY. Yeah. So?

TERRY. Ah, here they come.

> *(To the* **GUESTS**.*)*

May I have your attention please. Attention.

THANKS FOR ATTENDING OUR PARTY
WE'LL CHEER AS THE NEW YEAR BEGINS
LET'S HEAR ONE NOW
MAKE IT HEARTY
HERE THEY ARE
THE HILTON TWINS!

> *(***DAISY** *and* **VIOLET** *enter dressed in beautiful gowns.)*

DAISY & VIOLET.
WE HAVE HAD AN AMAZING YEAR
WE'RE SO GLAD OUR NEW FRIENDS ARE HERE

DAISY.
YOU COULD BE IN ROME

VIOLET.
BERLIN OR ST. TROPEZ

DAISY & VIOLET.
WE'RE PLEASED YOU'LL HELP US
TOAST NEW YEAR'S DAY

GUEST 1.
WHICH SIAMESE TWIN IS WHICH?

DAISY.
I'M DAISY.

VIOLET.
I'M VIOLET.

DAISY & VIOLET.
WE'RE NOT SIAMESE

GUEST 2.
THEN WHAT ARE YOU?

DAISY & VIOLET.
>TWINS
>WHO ARE CONJOINED

GUEST 3.
>WHATEVER YOU ARE
>DON'T YOU WANT TO BE NORMAL?

VIOLET.
>WHOEVER YOU ARE
>DON'T YOU?

DAISY.
>THE PARTY'S JUST BEGUN

VIOLET.
>ENJOY YOURSELVES

DAISY & VIOLET.
>HAVE FUN

>*[MUSIC NO. 16A: "WALTZ AND PROPOSAL."]*

>*(As the* **PARTY GUESTS** *dance,* **TERRY** *dances with* **DAISY**, **BUDDY** *with* **VIOLET**, *each couple having a private conversation.)*

DAISY. I adore New Year's Eve.

TERRY. It shows. You've never looked lovelier.

DAISY. This is the best one I've ever spent. Look at this place. These people.

TERRY. I'm so glad you're happy.

DAISY. Will you miss not being able to kiss your sweetheart at midnight?

TERRY. I'm not missing anyone. I'm just thrilled to be here with you.

>*(***TERRY** *dances closer to her as lights focus on* **BUDDY** *and* **VIOLET**.*)*

VIOLET. I hate New Year's Eve.

BUDDY. Me too!

VIOLET. It's the loneliest night of the year.

BUDDY. But you have no idea what it's like to be alone. When you've been out on your own your whole life, like me, always having someone by your side seems, I don't know, kinda nice.

> *(Music swells. They turn.* **TERRY** *and* **DAISY** *in the light.)*

TERRY. Violet seems so unhappy.

DAISY. Being the toast of the town is such a hardship for her.

TERRY. It's more than that, right?

DAISY. Well, you know, those school girl crushes – sometimes they're hard to get over.

> *(She looks at* **TERRY** *meaningfully as they turn and* **VIOLET** *and* **BUDDY** *come back into the light.)*

BUDDY. …after that, I was in and out of foster homes – never knew what to expect. So, I kept to myself.

VIOLET. Well, somehow we both survived.

BUDDY. And look where we are – with a bunch of swells in a fancy penthouse, hating New Year's Eve together. At least we'll have someone to kiss at midnight.

VIOLET. Right. A friendly peck on the cheek.

BUDDY. I'm thinking more than a peck.

VIOLET. Don't get carried away.

BUDDY. Why not? I am with my favorite girl.

VIOLET. You're just being nice.

BUDDY. Violet, you mean the world to me. Why don't we make this the one New Year's Eve we'll remember forever? I love you, you know.

VIOLET. Oh, please.

BUDDY. I do! And I know you love me. So now that I've said it, can I see a smile?

VIOLET. How's this?

> *(She smiles sarcastically.)*

BUDDY. Oh, come on. What do I have to do? Beg you on my knees?

VIOLET. Don't you dare.

BUDDY. I'm getting down on one knee and begging you to smile.

VIOLET. *(Stifling a laugh.)* You're embarrassing me.

BUDDY. And making you laugh a little?

TERRY. Hey, Buddy, what's going on over there? You look like you're proposing.

VIOLET. He's making fun of me.

BUDDY. I am not. Violet refuses to believe I love her.

DAISY. You do?

BUDDY. Of course.

TERRY. Then you are proposing.

VIOLET. He's not.

BUDDY. Would that make you happy?

DAISY. Couldn't hurt.

TERRY. What a story that would make.

DAISY. Can I be the maid of honor?

VIOLET. Stop it! All of you. Stop making fun of me.

BUDDY. Oh, Violet. No. Please don't cry. That's the last thing I want.

VIOLET. I'm sorry. I can't joke about this.

BUDDY. This isn't a joke.

> VIOLET, I LOVE YOU
> I DON'T KNOW HOW ELSE TO SAY IT
> I CHERISH EACH MOMENT I SPEND WITH YOU
> YOU SEE THINGS THE SAME WAY AS I DO

Violet Hilton, you make me so happy. Allow me to do the same. Marry me.

DAISY. *(After a pause, whispering to* **VIOLET***.)* If you don't say yes I'm going to have a heart attack that will kill us both.

BUDDY.

> WHAT ARE YOU WAITING FOR
> WHAT'S SO HARD?

VIOLET.

I'M CAUGHT BY SURPRISE
CAUGHT OFF-GUARD
NEVER EVEN HOPED FOR HAPPINESS
NOW I'M TRUSTING MY HEART
I'M SAYING YES, BUDDY, I'LL MARRY YOU

BUDDY.

NOW WE'LL NO LONGER BE ALONE

VIOLET.

NOT ALONE

BUDDY.

WE'VE GOT SOMEONE TO CALL
OUR OWN

VIOLET.

YOU'RE MY OWN

BUDDY & VIOLET.

I WILL MAKE YOU MY HOME
AND THAT IS WHERE I'LL STAY

TERRY.

LET'S MAKE IT PUBLIC
FOR NEW YEAR'S DAY

Ladies and gentlemen, the hour is upon us. And I've got big news with which to welcome the New Year. The lovely Miss Violet Hilton has accepted a marriage proposal from Mr. Buddy Foster!

(**GUESTS** *applaud.*)

I PROPOSE A TOAST
TO THESE LOVEBIRDS HERE
LET'S RAISE A GLASS
AND OUR VOICES IN CHEER
HERE'S TO A NEW LOVE

DAISY.

MAY IT BE TRUE LOVE

BUDDY & VIOLET.

ONE-MADE-FROM-TWO LOVE

TERRY, DAISY, BUDDY & VIOLET.
AND A HAPPY NEW YEAR

WOMEN & MEN.
HEAR, HEAR,
HEAR, HEAR!

ALL.
A HAPPY NEW YEAR!

> *(The* **GUESTS** *exchange embraces and kisses.)*

DAISY. *(To* **TERRY**.*)* Happy New Year.

> (**TERRY** *goes to kiss her, then backs off.)*

VIOLET. *(To* **BUDDY**.*)* Happy New Year.

> (**VIOLET** *and* **BUDDY** *kiss.)*

Jake, I'm finally getting married!

JAKE. Buddy's a lucky guy.

> (**GUESTS** *start exiting.)*

[MUSIC NO. 16B: "AULD LANG SYNE."]

ENSEMBLE SOLO.
SHOULD OLD
   AQUAINTANCE   **TERRY.**
BE FORGOT   Our guests are leaving.
                            You girls go make
                            your goodbyes

ADDITIONAL VOICES.   **ADDITIONAL VOICES.**
AND NEVER BROUGHT TO   SHOULD OLD
   MIND   ACQUAINTANCE BE
                           FORGOT

ADDITIONAL VOICES.
AND NEVER BROUGHT TO MIND

> (**GUESTS** *and* **DAISY** *and* **VIOLET** *exit.* **BUDDY** *and* **TERRY** *are left alone.)*

TERRY. That's a brilliant move, Buddy. It's the story of the year – the decade!

BUDDY. That's not why I did it. I can't stand to see her unhappy and now she won't be.

TERRY. Everyone benefits. The whole country will be rooting for you two.

BUDDY. Really? Well, they'd root twice as much for a double-wedding.

TERRY. You surprise me. First a threesome and now you want to up the ante?

BUDDY. That's not what I meant! It's just – Violet getting married is bound to be hard on Daisy.

TERRY. Daisy can take care of herself.

BUDDY. I'm sure she wants what Violet and I have.

TERRY. And what is that exactly?

BUDDY. Violet's my better half. She makes me the person I want to be. Doesn't Daisy do that for you?

TERRY. Hey! Mind your own business.

BUDDY. It's just…there's such an obvious connection between you two.

> (**BUDDY** *shrugs and exits.*)

Scene 3
Bare Stage

[MUSIC NO. 17: "A PRIVATE CONVERSATION."]

(**TERRY** *paces in frustration.*)

TERRY.
AN OBVIOUS CONNECTION
I TRIED SO HARD TO HIDE
COULDN'T EVEN SAY IT TO MYSELF
AN OBVIOUS CONNECTION
I TRIED TO PUSH ASIDE
INTO A CORNER
ON THE DARKEST SHELF

WE'LL NEVER BE ALONE
AND MY FEELINGS CAN'T BE SHOWN
SO I TRY TO IMAGINE AND REPLAY
ALL THE THINGS I'LL NEVER GET TO SAY

YOU'RE WRAPPED UP WITH ANOTHER
TANGLED AND ENTWINED
I INVENT A SEPARATION
IN THE PRIVATE CONVERSATION
IN MY MIND

I RESOLVE TO SAY IT ALL.
THEN I HEM AND HAW AND STALL.
FOR HOW CAN I COME CLEAN
OR CONFIDE
SOMEONE ELSE IS ALWAYS AT YOUR SIDE

I WANT
I WANT
I WANT TO TELL YOU
I WANT
I WANT
TO GET YOU ALONE
I NEED

I NEED
I NEED TO TELL YOU
I WANT YOU FOR MY OWN

IF WE COULD STEAL A MOMENT
WOULD YOU BE SO INCLINED
TO ACCEPT AN INVITATION
TO THE PRIVATE CONVERSATION
IN MY MIND

(**DAISY** *appears alone, upstage.*)

DAISY.

WHAT DO YOU WANT
TO SAY TO ME, TERRY?
TELL ME, THIS IS YOUR CHANCE
WHAT DO YOU NEED
TO SAY TO ME, TERRY?
DOES IT CONCERN ROMANCE?

HERE I AM
ALL ALONE
YOURS TO TAKE
SMOOTH ME OUT
CALM ME DOWN
STOP THE ACHE

DON'T HOLD BACK
DON'T HOLD OFF
HOLD ME TIGHT
DON'T OBJECT
LET'S CONNECT
LET'S UNITE

TERRY.

BUT YOU CAN'T LOSE YOUR SHADOW
THAT TIE YOU CAN'T UNBIND

DAISY.

YOU'VE MADE US ALL ALONE NOW

TERRY.

ALL ALONE
BUT ONLY IN MY MIND

DAISY.

 A MIND IS VERY PRIVATE
 WE OFTEN MEET IN MINE
 LET ME SHOW YOU WHAT WE DO THERE
 THE WAY WE KISS
 THE WAY WE INTERTWINE

 I WANT
 I WANT
 I WANT TO SHOW YOU

TERRY.

 SHOW ME WHAT?

DAISY.

 I WANT TO SHOW YOU DESIRE
 I NEED
 I NEED

TERRY

 I'M BURNING FOR YOU

DAISY.

 I KNOW YOU ARE ON FIRE

 WHY NOT BE BOLD
 I'M CRAZY ABOUT YOU
 I SAY IT WITH EV'RY GLANCE
 MY ARMS ARE COLD
 AND LAZY WITHOUT YOU
 COME ON
 WHY DON'T WE DANCE

  (Tentatively **DAISY** *turns* **TERRY** *toward her and puts his hand on her hip where her connection to* **VIOLET** *normally is. They begin to dance, slowly at first, then swirling around the stage.)*

TERRY.

 I WANT…
 I WANT…
 I WANT TO KEEP YOU

DAISY.

 KEEP ME WHERE?

(**VIOLET** *appears upstage.*)

TERRY.

I WANT YOU ALL FOR MY OWN
MY OWN…
MY OWN…

DAISY. *(Backing away from him.)*

YOU HAVE TO SHARE ME

TERRY.

OH NO
I WANT YOU ALONE

(**DAISY** *joins* **VIOLET** *and they disappear.*)

I IMAGINE US SO WELL
HOW YOU'D DANCE AND TASTE AND SMELL
I CAN IMAGINE
ME WITH YOU
BUT I DON'T HAVE THE GUTS
TO FOLLOW THROUGH

YOU'RE ONE HALF OF A COUPLE
THAT'S HOW YOU ARE DEFINED
AND MY ONLY CONSOLATION
IS THE PRIVATE CONVERSATION
IN MY MIND

(**BUDDY** *appears as the music suddenly turns jaunty.*)

Scene 4
On The Road

[MUSIC NO. 18: "ONE PLUS ONE EQUALS THREE."]

(**BUDDY** *sings and dances in a spotlight.*)

BUDDY.
    I NEVER SOUGHT THE SPOTLIGHT
    I STAYED BEHIND THE SCENES
    BUT THEN I MET A SWEETHEART
    WHO CHANGED MY OLD ROUTINES
    SHE PUT ME IN THE SPOTLIGHT
    NOW I'M A HAPPY PUP
    AND WHEN I COUNT MY BLESSINGS
    I FIND THEY ALL ADD UP TO

    ONE PLUS ONE EQUALS THREE
    MY BABY, HER SISTER AND ME
    THIS IS NOT WHAT I EXPECTED
    BUT MY BABY IS WELL-CONNECTED
    YOU CAN SEE WHY I ELECTED
    THIS ARITHMETIC WITH AN ODD KEY
    WHERE ONE PLUS ONE…EQUALS THREE

    SOME GUYS
    QUESTION HOW IT WILL WORK
    SOME WOMEN TITTER AND SMIRK
    IF YOU'RE WOND'RIN'
    WE'RE PLEASED TO DO
    THIS PREVIEW JUST FOR YOU

FEMALE ENSEMBLE. *(Bringing in a giant bed as Cherubs.)*
    WE'RE SENT BY CUPID
    LOVE CAN MAKE YOU STUPID
    LET US SHOW YOU HOW THEY'LL HAVE
    A SWEET HONEYMOON

BUDDY. *(Popping up in the bed.)*
    WELL…
    ONE PLUS ONE EQUALS …?

> (**DAISY** *and* **VIOLET** *pop up from under the "covers."*)

DAISY, VIOLET & FEMALE ENSEMBLE.
THAT'S GONNA BE
GONNA BE THREE

> (**BUDDY** *ducks below the "covers."*)

VIOLET & FEMALE ENSEMBLE.
HIS BABY

DAISY & FEMALE ENSEMBLE.
HER SISTER

BUDDY. *(Popping up.)*
AND DON'T FORGET ME

> (**BUDDY** *disappears below the "covers" leaving* **DAISY** *and* **VIOLET** *visible. They look at each other, then* **BUDDY**'s *head appears to one side.*)

DAISY.
AND, DON'T FORGET ME

> (**VIOLET** *ducks below covers, then her head appears next to* **BUDDY**'s *on the side.*)

VIOLET.
HEY, WHAT ABOUT ME?

> (**DAISY** *looks to her other side where* **RAY** *suddenly pops up.*)

RAY.
DOES IT HAVE TO BE THREE?

> (**DAISY** *ducks down leaving* **BUDDY** *and* **RAY** *looking at each other.*)

BUDDY.
ONE PLUS ONE

BUDDY, VIOLET, DAISY, RAY & ENSEMBLE.
EQUALS THREE!

> (**MALE ENSEMBLE** *enters as Cupids.*)

FEMALE ENSEMBLE.

    SHE'LL WEAR

    HER DREAM WEDDING GOWN

MALE ENSEMBLE.

    HE'LL BE

    THE TALK OF THE TOWN

ENSEMBLE. *(To* **BUDDY.***)*

    WHAT A HANDSOME, DELIGHTED GROOM

    THE PROUDEST IN THE ROOM!

       *(***BUDDY** *emerges from the "bed" dressed formally as the groom.* **VIOLET** *and* **DAISY** *enter,* **VIOLET** *in a wedding gown,* **DAISY** *dressed as a bridesmaid.)*

BUDDY.

    ONE PLUS ONE

DAISY, VIOLET, & ENSEMBLE.

    PLUS ONE

BUDDY.

    ONE PLUS ONE

DAISY, VIOLET, & ENSEMBLE.

    WHAT FUN!

BUDDY.

    ONE PLUS ONE

    MEANS MY BABY

VIOLET.	**CHERUBS & CUPIDS.**
I'M HIS BABY	HIS BABY

DAISY.

    I'M HIS BABY'S SISTER AND…

BUDDY.

    HER SISTER

ENSEMBLE.

    HIS BABY'S SISTER AND…

BUDDY.

    AND ME

ENSEMBLE.

    THAT EQUALS

VIOLET.
AND ME

ENSEMBLE.
THAT EQUALS

DAISY.
AND ME

ENSEMBLE.
THAT EQUALS

BUDDY, DAISY, VIOLET, & ENSEMBLE.
EQUALS THREE!

> *(Song ends. A* **CAMERAMAN** *has been filming the number.* **JAKE** *and* **TERRY** *are also nearby.)*

CAMERAMAN. Cut! That's a wrap.

TERRY. Did we get what we needed?

CAMERAMAN. Except for the two-shot of the bride and groom – the sister kept getting in the frame.

DAISY. Would it help if I cut off my head?

CAMERAMAN. She's a pistol!

DAISY. When are we going to see this newsreel in a theater?

JAKE. Right after bigamy becomes legal.

TERRY. Well, actually, I found a state that believes in the power of love and the rights of anyone who wants to wed.

VIOLET. And where is that?

TERRY. Texas!

CAMERAMAN. *(Starting to leave. To* **BUDDY.***)* Good luck, kid. Hope your rifle is double-barreled.

BUDDY. You think you're the first one to make that joke?

> *(The* **CAMERAMAN** *snickers as he exits.)*

TERRY. Hey, how about a little enthusiasm?

VIOLET. Texas?

DAISY. You promised we'd never have to go back there. Jake, could you get me some champagne?

(**JAKE** *ignores the request.*)

TERRY. This wedding is going to be the grand finale of the Texas Centennial – right on the fifty-yard line of the Cotton Bowl. You'll be on every front page in the nation!

DAISY. Oh, good. The whole country can joke about me.

TERRY. Daisy, I'm sorry people are so crude. But this is going to make you more famous than ever.

DAISY. Me? Is anyone going to get me that drink?

BUDDY. It's a bit early in the day.

DAISY. We are not getting married, so don't think you can tell me what to do!

TERRY. Daisy. Look at me. I didn't want to tell you this until I was absolutely certain, but I've been working on something that is going to make you very happy. I've been consulting with some of the best medical minds in the country. Their consensus is that the two of you could be successfully separated.

DAISY. Doctors have been telling us that our whole lives.

VIOLET. We were also told one of us might die.

TERRY. Just last month at Harvard surgeons operated on a pair of conjoined twins with a link twice as complex as yours. Tonight those twins sleep in separate bedrooms.

[MUSIC NO. 18A: "SEPARATION ANXIETY."]

Think of it! Violet, you could finally be like everyone else. Daisy, the whole world…at your feet.

DAISY. But, Terry, even if that were possible, we wouldn't be your big attraction if we're not together.

TERRY. Vaudeville is over – movies are where the action is. And where you should be!

DAISY. Us?

TERRY. No, you.

VIOLET. You know what I dream about? Sitting in a plush movie theater, holding my husband's hand – and watching you do all the work for a change.

DAISY. I couldn't go to Hollywood on my own.

TERRY. You wouldn't be on your own.

> (**TERRY** *kisses her – passionately – in front of everyone.*)

It's your decision, of course. But think of what this could mean – for all of us. Take it out!

> (**TERRY** *exits with* **BUDDY**.)

DAISY. I'm absolutely stunned.

VIOLET. I don't know what to think.

JAKE. It's a mistake! You shouldn't be messin' with what God created.

DAISY. We're God's mistakes.

JAKE. No you're not! You don't know your own worth.

DAISY. I finally have the chance to be loved.

JAKE. By someone who wants to change you completely?

VIOLET. Jake, you may be our closest friend, but this is between us.

[MUSIC NO. 19: "YOU SHOULD BE LOVED."]

JAKE.
I WANT YOUR HAPPINESS
MORE THAN ANYTHING
BUT I DON'T TRUST THIS

VIOLET.
WHAT DO YOU KNOW ABOUT IT?

JAKE.
I KNOW PLENTY
I KNOW HOW SOMEONE SHOULD LOVE YOU

VIOLET. And how is that?

> (*Pause.* **JAKE** *is momentarily paralyzed. Then HE takes a deep breath and starts*)

JAKE.
YOU SHOULD BE LOVED
BY SOMEONE WHO KNOWS YOU
WANTS YOU TO BLOSSOM
ALWAYS IS TRUE
YOU SHOULD BE CHERISHED
LIKE THE FIRST SIGN OF SPRINGTIME
YOU SHOULD BE LOVED

YOU SHOULD BE LOVED
WITH CONSTANT DEVOTION
HEART-POUNDING PASSION
FLOODING YOU THROUGH
YOU SHOULD BE TREASURED
LIKE A RUBY OR A DIAMOND
YOU SHOULD BE LOVED
IN THE WAY I LOVE YOU

ALL THROUGH THE YEARS
I'VE HELD OCEANS INSIDE
HELD BACK THE TEARS
AND THE WAVES AND THE TIDE
THE DAM HAD TO BURST
AND THE CURRENTS COLLIDE
WITH THE FLOOD OF EMOTION
I CAN NO LONGER HIDE

WE SHOULD BE CLOSE
AS STARS ARE TO HEAVEN
SHORELINE TO OCEAN
BIRDS TO THE BLUE
WE SHOULD BE COUPLED
WITH A LIFETIME CONNECTION
WE SHOULD BE JOINED
LIKE WE'RE ONE
AND NOT TWO
YES YOU SHOULD BE LOVED
IN THE WAY I LOVE YOU

VIOLET.
> JAKE, OF COURSE WE LOVE EACH OTHER
> LIKE A BROTHER AND SISTER
> FRIENDS TO THE END

JAKE.
> HAVEN'T YOU HEARD WHAT I'M SAYING?
> I AM IN LOVE WITH YOU

VIOLET.
> OH, JAKE, OH NO
> I NEVER THOUGHT, NEVER FELT

JAKE.
> WHAT I FELT?

VIOLET.
> I NEVER KNEW

JAKE.
> WELL NOW YOU DO
> I COULD MAKE YOU HAPPY

VIOLET.
> THE WORLD WON'T LET YOU

JAKE.
> I DON'T CARE ABOUT THEM – ONLY YOU
> WITH LOVE WE COULD RISE ABOVE
> THE WHISPERS AND STARES
> WE COULD CHALLENGE THE POWERS OF FATE
> MAKE THE BEST OF A BAD CIRCUMSTANCE
> IF YOU GIVE ME A CHANCE

VIOLET.
> I WANT TO BE LIKE EVERYONE ELSE
> I COULDN'T BEAR WHAT THEY WOULD SAY
> IF I LOVED YOU THAT WAY

I'm sorry, Jake, but I love Buddy.

> *(The* **TWINS** *exit.)*

JAKE.
      ONE OF THESE DAYS
      YOU WILL LOOK BACK IN SHAME
      YOU'LL BE ALONE
      AND YOU'LL KNOW YOU'RE TO BLAME
      YOU WILL REGRET
      HOW YOU PUSHED LOVE ASIDE
      WHEN YOU'RE MARRIED TO NOTHING
      WHEN YOU'RE MISERY'S BRIDE

      YOU SHOULD BE LOVED
      BY SOMEONE WHO WANTS YOU
      TRIES TO PROTECT YOU
      ALWAYS COMES THROUGH
      YOU SHOULD HAVE CHOSEN
      THE ONE WHO SUPPORTS YOU
      ALWAYS SUPPORTS YOU
      WHATEVER YOU DO
      YES, YOU SHOULD BE LOVED
      IN THE WAY I LOVE YOU

        (Scene change to the mid-way.)

Scene 5
The Texas Centennial

[MUSIC NO. 19A: "THE TEXAS CENTENNIAL."]

(Music takes us to the Texas Centennial. **TEXANS** *are scrambling for tickets for the upcoming wedding.)*

TEXAN 4.
CAN'T WAIT TO SEE THE BRIDE!

TEXAN 3.
I WAS THE FIRST IN LINE

TEXAN 12.
I'M NEXT

TEXAN 2.
NO, ME!

TEXAN 9.
GREAT SEATS

TEXAN 7.
GOT MINE!

TEXAN 5.
GONNA SEE THEM WED
WHAT AN EXHIBITION

TEXAN 10.
WHO WOULD MARRY SOMEONE
WITH THAT WEIRD CONDITION?

TEXAN 1 & TEXAN 4.
COMING SOON

TEXANS.
FOUR DAYS

TEXAN 12 & TEXAN 8.
HONEYMOON THREE WAYS

TEXANS.
YEAH!

TEXAN 1 & TEXAN 4.
I SWEAR!

TEXAN 11.

    MAYBE THEY CAN ALL SHARE

ALL.

    A BIG OLE
    ROOTIN', TOOTIN'
    VARMINT SHOOTIN'
    HOWLIN', HOOTIN'
    TEXAS SIDE SHOW!

       (**BUDDY** *is revealed.*)

[MUSIC NO. 20: "GREAT WEDDING SHOW."]

BUDDY.

    WHO'S THAT GUY I SEE
    ON EV'RY FRONT PAGE?
    LOOKS LIKE HE'S BEAMING WITH PRIDE
    ALL TOO SOON HE'LL TAKE
    HIS PLACE ON A STAGE
    POSING RIGHT NEXT TO HIS BRIDE
    BEGINNING A LIFE THAT HE'D RATHER SHARE
    WITH SOMEBODY NO ONE CAN KNOW
    INSTEAD HE'LL BE HALF OF
    A CURIOUS PAIR
    PART OF THIS GREAT
    WEDDING SHOW

TEXANS.

    ONLY THREE MORE DAYS!
    THIS STORY IS GREAT
    ARE THEY IN LOVE LIKE THEY SAY?
    HAVE THEY FOUND THE ONE
    THEIR PERFECT MATE
    OR IS IT ALL FOR DISPLAY?

TERRY.

    DAISY, I CAN FEEL
    THAT YOU WANT TO SHARE LIFE WITH ME
    HAVE THIS TANGLED KNOT BE UNTIED
    NOW IT'S UP TO YOU
    TO GET VIOLET TO AGREE
    YOU SHOULD BE FREE FROM HER SIDE

TEXANS.
>ONLY TWO MORE DAYS
>UNTIL THEY ARE WED
>EXCITEMENT CONTINUES TO GROW
>THREE OF THEM UP THERE
>AS TWO EXCHANGE VOWS
>OH WHAT A GREAT WEDDING SHOW
>>(**DAISY** *and* **VIOLET** *are revealed.*)

DAISY.
>I CAN'T STOP THINKING
>ABOUT TERRY'S PLAN
>I THINK WE SHOULD DO WHAT HE SAID

VIOLET.
>TERRY HAS LIED BEFORE
>HOW CAN YOU TRUST HIM NOW?
>WHAT IF WE'RE BEING MISLED?

DAISY.
>TERRY WOULDN'T LIE
>ABOUT SOMETHING LIKE THIS
>ONLY WANTS WHAT IS BEST FOR US BOTH

VIOLET.
>BUDDY LOVES ME
>LOVES ME FOR WHO I AM
>WANTS ME WITH ALL OF HIS HEART
>TERRY WOULD TEAR US APART

DAISY.
>TERRY LOVES ME
>WANTS ME ALL TO HIMSELF
>THE WAY YOU WANT BUDDY
>WE ALL COULD BE HAPPY AT LAST

VIOLET.
>SO MANY DOCTORS SAID
>HAVING AN OPERATION
>COULD END UP BEING FATAL
>FOR ONE OF US OR BOTH

DAISY.

    THAT WAS A DIFF'RENT TIME
    THE RISK IS NOT AS GREAT
    WE SHOULD TAKE THIS CHANCE
    TO BE ON OUR OWN

BUDDY.

    I GET SO LONELY
    IS THIS GOING TO CHANGE THAT?

TERRY.

    EV'RYONE HAD BETTER
    PLAY THIS MY WAY

DAISY.

    WE'D BE FREE

TERRY.

    FREE TO LOVE

BUDDY.

    FREE TO LIVE

DAISY.

    FREE TO FLY

TERRY.

    WHY NOT TRY?

VIOLET.

    WE MIGHT DIE!

DAISY.

    WE COULD FLY!

        (**TERRY** *directs* **DAISY***'s,* **VIOLET***'s and* **BUDDY***'s attention to a big wedding billboard featuring a photo of the three.*)

TERRY & BUDDY.	**TEXAN 4 & 8**.
FINALLY IT'S TIME	CAN'T WAIT TO SEE THE BRIDE
	TEXAN 9 & 12.
BIG DAY IS HERE	I WAS THE FIRST IN LINE
	TEXAN 5 & 6.
EVERYONE READY	I'M NEXT
	TEXAN 4 & 8.
TO GO	NO, ME!

TERRY.
  THE FUTURE

  LOOKS BRIGHT

  OUR PATH
  IS CLEAR
BUDDY.
  SEALING MY FATE
TEXANS.
  AH, AH

TEXAN 9 & 12.
  GREAT SEATS
TEXAN 1 & 10.
  GOT MINE!
TEXAN 5, 10, & 11.
  GONNA SEE 'EM WED
  WHAT AN EXHIBITION
TEXANS.
  AHH, AHH
BUDDY.
  WELL WORTH THE WAIT

DAISY, VIOLET, TERRY, BUDDY, TEXANS.
  OH WHAT A GREAT
  A GREAT
  WEDDING SHOW

  (Musical segue as lights change.)

Scene 6
The Texas Centennial Fairgrounds

[MUSIC NO. 21: "ATTRACTIONS RETURN."]

(**JAKE** *crosses into the scene. The* **HALF MAN**/**HALF WOMAN**, **GEEK** *and* **FORTUNE TELLER** *enter.*)

FORTUNE TELLER. Jake! We're so happy to see you!

JAKE. Bless my stars! Aren't you a sight for sore eyes.

FORTUNE TELLER. We came for the wedding.

HALF MAN/HALF WOMAN. To see the bride.

GEEK. And the Maid of Honor.

FORTUNE TELLER. I put together a bouquet for Violet.

HALF MAN/HALF WOMAN. I made her a veil.

GEEK. And I baked a cake.

JAKE. Of course you did. I've never forgotten your birthday cakes. So how's the sideshow these days?

FORTUNE TELLER. You didn't hear?

HALF MAN/HALF WOMAN. Completely shut down.

GEEK. First the girls left, then do-gooders tried to save us from being exploited.

HALF MAN/HALF WOMAN. All they saved us from was being fed.

GEEK. We couldn't find work anywhere. But now the three of us have a bakery.

HALF MAN/HALF WOMAN. I take care of ordering supplies, the accounts –

FORTUNE TELLER. – and I handle the customers at the front of the store.

GEEK. She tells fortunes in the back.

FORTUNE TELLER. People don't live by cake alone.

HALF MAN/HALF WOMAN. We're so happy for Violet.

GEEK. She's our inspiration. They both are!

JAKE. I just hope they get everything they deserve.

FORTUNE TELLER. Of course they will!
    I'VE LOOKED INTO MY CRYSTAL BALL.
    A ROSY FUTURE IS IN SIGHT
JAKE.
    THAT'S WHAT YOU ALWAYS SAY
FORTUNE TELLER.
    AND, DARLING
    I'M ALWAYS RIGHT
  Come on, let's go see our girl get married.

      *(***ATTRACTIONS*** *exit with* **JAKE.***)*

      (Scene change.)

Scene 7
Stadium Dressing Area

*(**DAISY** and **VIOLET** are dressed for the wedding.)*

VIOLET. I can't believe how nervous I am.

*(**DAISY** is silent.)*

You love a big crowd, but for me the thought of all those people is terrifying.

(No response.)

Daisy, can we just get through the ceremony and then decide about the operation?

DAISY. Of course. Why don't we discuss that tonight – during the honeymoon?

VIOLET. Don't be a brat.

*(**SIR** enters.)*

SIR. What's wrong? You girls should be happy for each other

VIOLET. How'd you get back here?

DAISY. Jake!

SIR. It's your big wedding day, isn't it?

DAISY. You weren't invited.

SIR. I bought my ticket like the rest of your guests – all those close friends you've never met. I spent my last cent to be here.

DAISY. What do you want?

SIR. When you girls left, I lost everything. I need a job. Please, I'll do anything…you know I'm a hard worker. Daisy, wouldn't you like to boss me around for a change?

*(**JAKE** enters.)*

JAKE. You are not welcome here.

SIR. Jake. Looking quite the gentleman.

JAKE. Do I need to throw you out?

SIR. No, no… Time to take my seat. Just having a chat. Congratulations, Violet.

     (**SIR** *exits.*)

JAKE. We can't let him ruin this day, can we? Violet, I always knew you'd make a beautiful bride.

VIOLET. You're very kind, Jake.

JAKE. It's hard for me to say this. But after the wedding, I'll be heading out.

DAISY. What do you mean?

JAKE. Time to move on. Guy I know has a little club in Chicago. Needs someone to work with performers. Thanks to you, I got experience with that.

DAISY. But we need you!

VIOLET. Please don't go.

JAKE. Violet, I've never been able to say no to you. But this time I have to.

     (**TERRY** *and* **BUDDY** *enter.*)

TERRY. Happy wedding day!

BUDDY. What a crowd out there!

VIOLET. Buddy, it's bad luck if you see me before the ceremony.

TERRY. Oh, who believes those old wives' tales anymore?

VIOLET. Get out, Buddy.

TERRY. Is something wrong?

DAISY. Jake's leaving. He's got a job in Chicago.

TERRY. Well, Jake, your timing could be better, but… congratulations. I'm glad you could find work somewhere.

JAKE. I've worked my whole life, Terry. Not just for you and the girls. Buddy, you'd better be good to Violet. She deserves better.

[MUSIC NO. 22: "BUDDY'S CONFESSION."]

JAKE. *(Cont.)*

> IF YOU HURT HER I WILL HUNT YOU DOWN

BUDDY. Jake, what has happened to you? I always thought of us as friends.

DAISY.

> HE LOVES HER
> HE TRULY DOES

JAKE.

> I DO, BUDDY
> MORE THAN YOU EVER CAN
> SO COME ON
> TELL THE TRUTH
> BE A MAN

BUDDY. *(Pause.)*

> HE'S RIGHT, VIOLET
> YOU DESERVE BETTER

TERRY. Buddy!

BUDDY.

> I'VE TRIED
> BUT I'M PLAYING A PART
> I'VE TRIED AND IT'S BREAKING MY HEART

VIOLET.

> YOU DON'T LOVE ME?

BUDDY.

> I DO, VIOLET
> BUT NOT THE WAY YOU WANT
> I'M NOT THE RIGHT ONE FOR YOU

VIOLET.

> BUT YOU'RE THE ONE I LOVE

BUDDY.

> YOU SHOULD BE LOVED
> BY SOMEONE LIKE JAKE
> SOMEBODY STRONG WHO'S ABLE TO TAKE
> WHATEVER COMES ALONG

I'M NOT READY YET
FOR A STEP WE'D BOTH REGRET
IF ONLY I'D KNOWN IT BEFORE
HURTING YOU THIS WAY
HURTS ME EVEN MORE

TERRY. *(Grabbing his arm.)* Buddy, get a hold of yourself!

BUDDY. I have.

DAISY. Violet, don't cry. It's for the best.

VIOLET. How can you say that?

DAISY. Buddy, why don't you tell her what's really going on?

BUDDY. Daisy, this is between your sister and me.

DAISY. She may be blind, but I'm not. You've got it easy, Buddy. Unlike a lot of us you can hide what makes you different.

TERRY. Daisy.

VIOLET. Don't be cruel.

*(A well-dressed **MAN** enters.)*

BROWNING. Excuse me.

TERRY. No one's allowed back here!

BROWNING. Well, I'm quite sure I am.

TERRY. Who the hell are you?

BROWNING. Tod Browning from MGM.

TERRY. Mr. Browning!

DAISY. The movie director?

BROWNING. You must be the Hilton Sisters. Lovely. Lovely.

*(To **BUDDY**.)*

And you – you're the groom?

VIOLET. He's not. The wedding is off.

TERRY. Violet.

BROWNING. Did I hear you correctly?

VIOLET. Yes, you did.

BROWNING. What a shame. I came all the way from Hollywood. I intended to offer you roles in my new film.

DAISY. We can still be in your film.

BROWNING. I don't know…without the publicity from the wedding…

[MUSIC NO. 22A: "MARRY ME, TERRY."]

DAISY.

I HAVE A SOLUTION
MARRY ME, TERRY

TERRY.

WITH THE WHOLE WORLD
EXPECTING A DIFFERENT PAIR?

DAISY.

THEY'RE EXPECTING
THE WEDDING OF A SIAMESE TWIN
THEY WON'T CARE

BROWNING.

SMART GIRL

DAISY.

MARRY ME, TERRY
IT MAKES SO MUCH SENSE
I KNOW YOU WANT ME
JUMP OFF THE FENCE
THE CROWD WANTS A WEDDING
THE BRIDE HAS WITHDRAWN
MARRY ME, TERRY
THE SHOW MUST GO ON

TERRY. I can't wait to marry you, Daisy – right after the operation.

BROWNING. What operation?

TERRY. You know, Mr. Browning, it's uncanny you showing up like this. I've been planning to pursue a movie career for Daisy and I've found doctors who can safely separate her from Violet.

BROWNING. Separate? No, I'm interested in them as they are.

TERRY. What?

VIOLET. As we are?

BROWNING. Of course. There's no one like you. You're unique.

DAISY. That's what you said, Terry, when we first met.

TERRY. A lot has changed since then. Mr. Browning, thank you for your interest. But I've got other plans for the girls.

BROWNING. And who the hell are you?

TERRY. Who am I? I'm the guy who made this all happen. I am the only reason you're here. Without me these girls would be in some shithole tent in Texas instead of a stadium filled with 60,000 people waiting for a wedding that is going to happen –

    (Crossing to **BUDDY**.*)*

as soon as you pull your pansy-ass together and marry this…this…

    (Stops, unable to finish.)

DAISY. This what? Say it. Mr. Browning, there's not going to be an operation. We came into this world together…

VIOLET. …and we'll leave it the same way.

BROWNING. What about the wedding? Still planning to cancel.

VIOLET. No. My sister was prepared to sacrifice a lot for my dream. I'm happy to return the favor.

BUDDY. Do I have anything to say about this?

VIOLET. Buddy, it's just for show. And you'll be famous.

DAISY. She's right. We can all meet for lunch in Hollywood and pretend we're friends.

BUDDY. *(To* **VIOLET**.*)* We wouldn't have to pretend would we?

(**VIOLET** *shakes her head.* **BUDDY** *exits.*)

DAISY. Mr. Browning, you've got your movie stars.

TERRY. We can discuss the contract after the ceremony.

DAISY. Oh that won't be necessary.

TERRY. Daisy, please don't confuse business with emotion.

DAISY. I'm not confused.

VIOLET. We don't want to work with you.

DAISY. Good-bye Terry.

(**TERRY** *exits.*)

Mr. Browning, what's the name of our film?

BROWNING. "Freaks."

[MUSIC NO. 23: "I WILL NEVER LEAVE YOU."]

(*He exits. Then* **JAKE** *follows.*)

VIOLET.

WHAT HAVE WE DONE?

DAISY.

LEARNED THE TRUTH

VIOLET.

CLOSED A DOOR

DAISY.

OPENED MORE

VIOLET.

I'M SCARED, DAISY.

DAISY.

OF WHAT?

VIOLET.

BEING ALONE.

DAISY.

BUT YOU'RE NOT
YOU NEVER HAVE BEEN
IF WE STOOD ON OUR TIPTOES
WE COULD PEEK OVER THE SILL

AND ONCE IN A WHILE WE WOULD SEE A GIRL
SLOWLY WALKING UP THE HILL

VIOLET.

AND WE'D THINK WHAT A SAD SITUATION
TO BE OUTSIDE ON YOUR OWN

DAISY.

TO GO THROUGH THE DAY
WITH NO PLAYMATE

VIOLET.

TO GO THROUGH LIFE ALL ALONE

DAISY & VIOLET.

I WILL NEVER LEAVE YOU
I WILL NEVER GO AWAY
WE WERE MEANT TO SHARE EACH MOMENT
BESIDE YOU IS WHERE I WILL STAY
EVERMORE AND ALWAYS
WE'LL BE ONE THOUGH WE'RE TWO
FOR I WILL NEVER LEAVE YOU

DAISY.

WHEN THE DAY IS FILLED WITH SHADOWS
THAT STRETCH INTO THE NIGHT

VIOLET.

I AM FILLED WITH YOUR SWEET COMFORT
LIKE MORNING FILLS WITH LIGHT

DAISY & VIOLET.

I WILL NEVER LEAVE YOU
I WILL NEVER GO AWAY
WE WERE MEANT TO SHARE EACH MOMENT
BESIDE YOU IS WHERE I WILL STAY
EVERMORE AND ALWAYS
WE'LL BE ONE THOUGH WE'RE TWO
FOR I WILL NEVER LEAVE YOU

DAISY.

OK, I WILL NEVER LEAVE YOU

VIOLET.

I WILL NEVER LEAVE YOU

DAISY.

    I WILL

DAISY & VIOLET.

    NEVER GO AWAY

    WE WERE MEANT TO SHARE EACH MOMENT

DAISY.

    BESIDE YOU IS WHERE I WILL STAY

VIOLET.

    THAT'S WHERE I WILL STAY

DAISY.

    EVERMORE AND ALWAYS

VIOLET.

    EVERMORE WE'LL BE ONE THO' WE'RE TWO

DAISY.

    ONE THO' WE'RE TWO

DAISY & VIOLET.

    FOR...

    I WILL NEVER

    I WILL NEVER

    I WILL NEVER LEAVE YOU

    [MUSIC NO. 24: "FINALE: WEDDING/ FREAKS REPRISE."]

    (**DAISY** *and* **VIOLET** *pivot and walk upstage. The* **GEEK**, **FORTUNE TELLER** *and* **HALF MAN/ HALF WOMAN** *give* **VIOLET** *a bouquet and veil. Then* **DAISY** *and* **VIOLET** *pivot again and cross downstage as in a wedding procession.*)

Scene 8
The Cotton Bowl

*(**DAISY** and **VIOLET** walk at a processional pace.)*

VIOLET.

DAISY, CAN YOU HEAR WHAT I'M THINKING?

DAISY.

YES, CLEARLY AS THO' YOU SPOKE

VIOLET.

GIVE ME STRENGTH
I FEEL MY SPIRITS SINKING

DAISY.

TRY TO LAUGH
THIS IS THE BIGGEST JOKE
WE HAVE SEEN THE WORLD

VIOLET.

AND IT'S SEEN US

DAISY.

WE HAVE CAUSED A SCENE

VIOLET.

WE HAVE MADE A FUSS
ARE WE EVER TO LEARN
WHY WE'VE LIVED AS TWO?

DAISY.

PROB'LY NOT
BUT I'M THANKFUL

DAISY & VIOLET.

IT'S BEEN WITH YOU

*(**BUDDY** enters and takes his place as the groom.
He and **VIOLET** exchange rings and kiss.)*

DAISY.   **ENSEMBLE.**

COME LOOK AT THE   AH AH *(etc.)*
   FREAKS

VIOLET.

BEFORE THEY'RE ANTIQUES

DAISY & VIOLET.

COME AND GIVE THEM A STRONG OVATION
AN ACCLAMATION BUT NO CRITIQUES

DAISY.

SEE WHAT HOLLYWOOD SEEKS

DAISY & VIOLET.

COME LOOK AT THE FREAKS

> (*The set transforms to a sound stage, much hustle and bustle as the "FREAKS" poster seen at the beginning flies in.*)

DAISY, VIOLET & COMPANY.

AH, AH, AH
AH, AH, AH, AH AH, AH, AH, AH
AH, AH, AH

ASSISTANT DIRECTOR. Where's the tea guy?!

> (**SIR** *rushes on with two cups of tea, spills some, wipes it up.*)

Quiet everyone. Mr. Browning is arriving on the set.

> (**TOD BROWNING** *enters. He is directing "FREAKS."*)

DAISY, VIOLET AND COMPANY.

AH, AH, AHHH

BROWNING. Come look at the freaks!

ALL.

SIDE BY SIDE
CURIOSITY SATISFIED
COME AND GIVE THEM A STRONG OVATION
AN ACCLAMATION
BUT NO CRITIQUES
SEE LOVE GLORIFIED
SEE LOVE GLORIFIED

BARITONES.

SEE LOVE GLORIFIED

TENORS.

SEE LOVE GLORIFIED

WOMEN.
  SEE LOVE GLORIFIED
TWO WOMEN & FOUR MEN.
  SEE LOVE GLORIFIED
  COME HEAR HOW LOVE SPEAKS
  COME LOOK AT THE FREAKS!
  [MUSIC NO. 25: "BOWS AND EXIT MUSIC."]

The End.

CPSIA information can be obtained
at www.ICGtesting.com
Printed in the USA
LVHW051621070219
606771LV00022B/320/P